THE FREE TRADERS

The Free Traders deal fur and whisky, debouching their way through the Canadian northern territories. Pitted against them are the country's soldier-police, the Northwest Mounted. Lee Anderson, Royal Canadian Mounted Police sergeant, is on a mission to find a man wanted for murder twenty-five years ago. But when he and a mysterious woman are thrown down a cliff by a dynamite explosion, her memory disappears from the shock, and they find themselves in a wilderness pursued by the Free Traders — who are bent on killing Lee and capturing the woman.

VICTOR ROUSSEAU

THE FREE TRADERS

Complete and Unabridged

LINFORD
Leicester

First published in Great Britain

First Linford Edition
published 2019

A catalogue record for this book is available
from the British Library.

ISBN 978–1–4448–4234–0

Published by
F. A. Thorpe (Publishing)
Anstey, Leicestershire

Set by Words & Graphics Ltd.
Anstey, Leicestershire
Printed and bound in Great Britain by
T. J. International Ltd., Padstow, Cornwall

This book is printed on acid-free paper

1

Sergeant Anderson Rides
into Little Falls

Lee Anderson, sergeant in the Royal
Canadian Mounted Police, had been
leading his horse up the last hill. Now he
stopped at the top, letting the animal
snatch a few blades of the sparse grass
that grew among the ferns and raspberry
brambles beside the cart track.

There were, perhaps, thirty-three or
-four years to his credit. His rather lined,
deeply sunburned face and throat con-
trasted markedly with the edging of white
flesh at the V-top of his open shirt. Lee, in
his prospector's clothing, appeared to be
typically one of those reserved, quiet,
self-contained men whom the north
breeds.

His rather heavy horse, a combination
of pack and saddle, was well-laden behind
the rolled blankets that formed a parapet

across its shoulders.

Lee inhaled with delight the warm, steamy exhalations of the earth, rich with the added debris of the year. He turned and looked forward, beyond the settlement of Little Falls lying at the foot of the slope in front of him, the last of the settlements on his side of Stony Range. It was an unkempt, untidy little place created by the advent of the lumber companies a few years before, and straggling among the knee-high stumps of what had been virgin forest within the decade.

After his belated return from France, only to find the old Northwest mounted, of which he had been a member, merged in the new Dominion body, Lee himself had been stationed at Manistree. He had been in the police eight years before the war. It was the only life that appealed to him. His service had expired during his term at the front, but his first act on returning had been to rejoin. Inspector Crawley had sent for him a few days later.

'Anderson,' he said, 'I want you to be ready to start for Stony Range in the morning to pick up a man named Pelly. He's on the 'wanted' list — headed it for some time, in fact. I guess you don't know anything about the case, though.'

'No, sir. It must have happened while I was in France.'

'Oh, it happened a deuce of a time before you went to France, Anderson. Twenty-five years ago, more or less. Might have left the poor devil alone, especially as he's been a fugitive so long. But it's murder, Sergeant, and — well, the new police have got to show themselves just as efficient bloodhounds as the old force. The papers in the case have just come through Ottawa.

'This man Pelly appears to have killed a man in Toronto in the nineties for insulting his wife. Those details are not given. It appears a tip came down some time ago that Pelly has been living in the Siston Lake region, on the other side of Stony Range, for a good many years. Pelly appears to have got wind of this and made a quick getaway. Now the word's come in that he's been seen in the district . . . may be true or false.

'Probably it won't be possible to convict now. If it is possible, I don't suppose he'll get much of a sentence. But headquarters are anxious that we should establish our prestige by getting after him — to show that we're on the job as our predecessors were. I want you to ride in, and, if he's alive, pick him up and bring him back with you.'

Anderson saluted. He was about to leave the office when the inspector called him back. 'Stop a moment, Sergeant. You can guess that this man Pelly was probably betrayed by someone with a grudge against him. I suppose you know that the Free Traders opened up at Siston Lake during the war?'

The Free Traders, as Anderson knew, were a gang of liquor men organized from Montreal, sending agents far and wide into the Indian lands, debauching and corrupting. The Free Traders dealt in human souls as well as fur and whisky; they were the most iniquitous thing that had so far entered the northern territories.

'There's a man named Jim Rathway

who seems to be handling their work for 'em up there. Ten to one his gang's mixed up with this Pelly matter in some way. Perhaps they're out for Pelly's head because he wouldn't stand in with 'em. On the other hand, there's the chance that he's in with 'em and someone else tipped us off. In that case you'll find yourself up against the organization.

'This Rathway's believed to have been running liquor under various aliases for years, and there's ugly rumor about happenings at an Indian camp in the Far North, where the Free Traders have another post at Lake Misquash. They've got to be a big factor during the years of the war — so big that we're not going to tackle 'em until we're ready to launch a general campaign against 'em.

'You'll remember not to butt in if you find 'em selling liquor, but pick up Pelly as quietly as possible, and take notes if you get the chance, on what's going on at Siston Lake.

'You've got carte blanche, and you'll take a covering warrant from the stipendiary to use in any way you see fit.

And take all the time you want, because there'll be nothing doing till spring. But don't let 'em get wise to your job. So you'll leave your uniform behind you, Sergeant, and conduct your inquiries as inconspicuously as possible. And in a case like this, one man's better than two. That's why I'm sending you alone.

'Finally, you'll bear in mind that Pelly's arrest comes first. Soon as you locate him, bring him out of the range.'

At dawn, Lee was upon the road.

There had been rumors — recurrent rumors of a gold find in Stony Range that summer, but the nearer Lee got to the range, the less explicit the news became. He passed a number of men on their way south, morose and sullen, but ready enough to pour out their grievance that a summer's prospecting had failed to show even a trace of color anywhere. Lee had listened to their stories and then gone on, leaving the impression that he was a prospector on a belated journey to the range.

And now at last the range lay in front of him, uplifting its wild peaks into the glory of the autumn sunset. Lee felt his heart uplifted too. This was life at its most zestful — the world spaces, and the hunting of the king of all created beings: man.

So, leading his horse, Lee passed down the long slope toward the settlement of Little Falls. Soon he was abreast of the first shacks, set in the clearings among the stumps. Then came rows of uniformly ugly wooden cottages, a small mission church with a tin roof, a bank, and a small hotel announcing itself by a dilapidated shingle.

Lee fastened his horse to the hitching post in front and entered. On the right of the interior passage was the dining-room, on the left the parlor, with the furniture piled up in corners and the floor strewn with duffle-bags and blankets.

A passage ran past a flight of rickety stairs, and from a room at the end of this came the clamor of voices. Here Lee found the bar, packed tight and running wide open. Behind the mahogany stood a fat and cynical-looking landlord.

'How about a room and stabling for the

night?' asked Lee.

The landlord slid a schooner of beer from one end of the bar to the middle and turned to Lee, his fat body quivering, apparently with mirth, though his face did not relax anything of its solemn, cynical aspect

'Stabling? You said it. Room? You can have six foot by four of the parlor floor, stranger,' he answered.

'Pretty full, eh?'

'Fuller 'n hell's full of fire-logs.'

'Logging crews signing up?'

'Loggin', nothin'. Town's full of these here fool guys that's been prospectin' Stony Range all summer. Got cold feet all at once and all quit together. Feeling pretty sore over it, I guess. You ain't aimin' to start for the range yourself this time of year?'

'I guess there'll be time to wash a few pans of dirt,' answered Lee. 'Then maybe I'll board my horse here and trap a bit this winter.'

He led his horse into the stable, gave it some corn and racked out a bale of hay, and carried his blankets back to the hotel parlor, where he staked out a sleeping claim upon the floor.

A small black boy carrying a large bell came out of the kitchen and began to ring it, swaying to and fro with a cheerful grin, as if he were tied to the clapper. At the sound of the cracked tones, the men begun to struggle out of the bar into the dining-room, where they took their seats on benches either side of a long table covered with a stained, tattered oilcloth on which were placed cheap knives, forks, spoons and plates. Next appeared a thick set young squaw who began to hand out portions of a greasy dinner consisting of suspicious meat, beans, and potatoes that had apparently been frozen to death in bed.

Lee, who had taken a seat opposite the door, surveyed the other guests with that quiet watchfulness which was a part of his nature as well as of his training. For the most part, he summed them up as being of the average prospector type. Among them, however, appeared to be a few of those hard-bitten characters who are to be found in every gold rush. Most of them had been drinking freely, and all seemed embittered by their experiences of the summer. They were freely cursing their ill-luck.

Lee's attention was first drawn to the two men who were seated opposite him by the fact that they took no part in this chorus of denunciation. A glance showed him that they were not prospectors, and that the understanding between them was an intimate one. One was a short, thick-set, muscular red-haired man with one of the hardest and most repulsive faces that Lee had ever seen. The other, apparently his partner, was a huge mixed-race man with a great muscular torso.

'If I had that guy here what started that yarn about the gold in Stony Range — ' began a man on Lee's right.

'Ah, for the love of Mike, cut out that spiel, Bill!' shouted another across the table. 'D'you think you're the only real fool's been summerin' in the range?'

'Old Pelly never found no gold mine. He was cracked about it. If he had, wouldn't others have got wise to it with half the district hangin' about the range spyin' on him?'

'Nobody knows what happened to him, do they?'

'Just disappeared. Mebbe he had a stroke in the woods or somethin'. Nobody's seen nor heard of him this good while past.'

Lee absorbed this conversation without feeling that he had got very far. Pelly had discovered a problematical gold mine. He had disappeared; it began to seem probable that the report of his return was false. If these men had been prospecting the range all the summer, it was probable that if Pelly had returned to the vicinity, they would have heard of it. In which case, someone would have corrected the statement that nothing was known about it.

While he listened, Lee noticed that the two men opposite him were likewise taking in every word. The bigger man was obviously under the influence of liquor, and his little companion was not only watching the company but also watching him. At times he would turn and whisper in his companion's ear. And once, in his close scrutiny of the company, he turned his gaze on Lee.

For a moment Lee felt chilled by the eyes of the little red-haired man. They were pale grey, glassy, venomous. They looked like a snake's eyes. Lee, though his gaze was as steady as the other's, did not like the look of the little red-haired man.

The conversation drifted. By twos and threes, the men began to make their way back to the bar. Lee had risen from the table and left the dining-room, intending to take a smoke on the stoop, when he heard a feminine voice, and found himself staring in surprise at a woman who had just come in and was in conversation with the landlord.

For this was not in the least the type of woman whom one might look for in such a place as Little Falls.

2

A Woman Rides into the Range

She was perhaps twenty-two or -three, slender, of medium height with clear, grey, fearless eyes, and hair of pale brown with gold flecks in it, coiled up loosely about her head. Her open mackinaw revealed an almost boyish figure, slender and long-waisted. She wore corduroy breeches and riding gaiters; and there was about her that hardly definite, but unmistakable air of breeding that crops out in such unexpected places along the Anglo-Saxon frontier.

From a respectful distance the men were staring at her, each asking Lee's unspoken question as to what such a woman was doing in Little Falls. That she was riding into the range was evident. Had she been riding out, the men would have known of her. But — whose daughter was she? There was no one in the now deserted range to whom she could be going. The only possible destination might be the Moravian mission on the other side. But there were no women at the mission.

'Well, you see, miss,' the landlord was saying, 'we're pretty well filled up so far as rooms is concerned. But the wife's over to Old Landing fer a few days, an' I guess you can have our room till she comes home. It's the first room on the right at the top of the stairs. You just walk up and make yourself comfortable, miss, and I'll take your horse into the stable and see that he gets fed and watered. And supper's ready.'

'Thank you, but I had mine on the road. And I shall be going on early in the morning.'

By now, the crowd of ex-prospectors had formed a wide circle about the woman, standing as far as the passage would permit, staring and scrutinizing her frankly, and looking sheepishly away whenever her unembarrassed glance fell upon any of them. Lee, hearing a muttering behind him, turned to see the big muscular man staring at the woman and whispering excitedly to his companion. His red-headed partner was tugging at his arm as if to restrain him.

'You damn fool, Pierre!' Lee heard him expostulate.

Suddenly the man shook off the other's grip and lurched forward. Planting himself in front of the woman, he leaned toward her with an expression on his face that brought the blood into her cheeks. Before he could utter a word, however, Lee stepped quietly into the breach with that instinctive air of authority which he retained, despite the shedding of his uniform.

'That'll be all,' he said crisply.

The big man turned on him and broke into a string of oaths. 'Say, whadya mean?' he shouted. 'You don't know me. He don't know who he's talking to, eh, Shorty? I'm Pierre Cauchon.' He doubled a brawny forearm. 'Say, young feller, you see this? There ain't no man either side of the range can say 'that'll be all' to Pierre Cauchon. You think you can fight, mebbe?'

Lee, mindful of the rigid code of conduct that bound him, shook his head. 'I never fight if I can help it,' he answered.

The two men snickered, and there came a murmur of disgust from the crowd, which, till that moment, had been decidedly favorable to Lee.

Pierre turned about. 'He never fight if he can help it,' he jeered. 'You hear that, boys?' He turned to Lee again. 'Mebbe you like to set up the drinks, then?' he inquired blandly.

'I don't drink,' answered Lee with complete equanimity.

'Well, whadya think of that?' cried Pierre to the crowd again. 'He don't fight an' he don't drink. You sure are one damn four-flusher.' He grinned belligerently in Lee's face.

Lee, relieved to see, without turning his head, that the woman had taken the opportunity to slip away, returned Pierre's glare openly. The man was poising himself ready to strike, but something in Lee's aspect, some uncertainty, the inability to size him up, checked him. Perhaps he sensed how quickly Lee's right arm, hanging negligently before him, would rise to the defensive; perhaps he did not like the look of Lee's left.

He took refuge in irony. 'Well, whadya think of him, boys?' he demanded again of the men, who had formed a close circle around the pair. 'He don't fight an' he got the nerve to say 'that'll be all' to Pierre Cauchon. No, by God, I guess you know better than to fight,' he continued, adding a foul epithet; and, grinning, he lurched insolently past toward the bar, shouldering Lee as he passed.

He looked back for an instant to see whether the other would accept the provocation, and, seeing that he allowed no signs of doing so, he went on his way with Shorty. The crowd gave Lee the once-over contemptuously. It had no love for the bully, but an individual without the fighting instinct was not supposed to pose as a lady's champion and then back down. The minds of the prospectors were too obtuse to see that Lee had simply been satisfied with gaining his point and enabling the woman to get away unmolested.

He interested himself in speculating who the woman was. She was almost certainly going to the mission; there could be no other destination. Perhaps he would see her again. He thought of the possibility quite without emotion. He ceased to think of her, and, tired after the day's ride, began to doze.

He was awakened when the men began to stagger into the parlor. Nearly all of them were drunk, some were rolling drunk, and, after sporadic, noisy altercations, they were soon sprawled out like logs all over the floor and snoring loudly.

He was just falling asleep again when the sound of a name, whispered almost in his ear, startled him into instant wakefulness. Lee recognized the voice as that of Pierre Cauchon.

For a moment or two, he could not imagine from where the man was speaking. Then he discovered that the voice came from the other side of the large, empty stove which stood at his head, a little out from the wall. His face and Pierre's were separated, therefore, by no more than the circumference of the metal container, though Pierre, of course, did not guess that Lee lay on the other side of it, nor that he would he likely to have any particular interest in what he was saying.

But the name that had startled Lee into wakefulness was that of Pelly. His subconscious, alert through slumber, had caught it and communicated the warning.

Before Lee had quite attuned his ears to catch Pierre's remark, Shorty, the other man, broke in: 'You fool, Pierre, you nearly give the game away tonight for sure. You ain't got no sense at all, buttin' in like that and frightenin' her away. You didn't s'pose she'd got our photographs in her pocket, did you? The trouble with you is you can't hold yer liquor.'

Pierre growled: 'I didn't have no chance to say a word before that four-flusher butted in. I wish I'd beat him up now. Mebbe I'll get the chance in the mornin'.'

'Well, and why didn't you? I'll tell you why. Because you saw he ain't no four-flusher. He's tough, that feller is, an' he was watchin' you like a cat. Don't you make no mistake about that. And it's lucky you didn't get no chance to spill what you was goin' to, or you'd sure have scared the woman away . . . You listen here,' he continued, 'you keep out of this tomorrow till she's gone, and then we can ride hard and catch up with her at sundown and explain that we're friends of hers.'

Their voices became inarticulate. Lee strained his ears to catch the import of their conversation, but he could hear nothing but the low whisper of their voices.

'Well, I guess you're right, Shorty,' said Pierre after a while. 'We got to see she don't give us the slip, though.'

Shorty snickered and whispered something to which the other clucked approval. 'She can't, neither,' he said. 'There's only one way into the range, an' when we got her there, we got her where we want her.'

No more was said, and soon the snoring from the other side of the stove indicated that the pair had succumbed to sleep. But all desire for sleep was banished from Lee's brain.

There was the alternative of two courses of action: he could warn the woman in the morning, placing himself at her disposal; or he could keep her more or less in sight during his journey the following day, with a view to protecting her from the pair of ruffians whenever they made their appearance. But he could not afford to take any action which would give the clue to his status and activities; and apart from that, he wanted to keep in touch with the two men, in case they could furnish any clue to Pelly's whereabouts — if he were alive.

Sometime early in the morning, he fell into a restless slumber, from which he was partly aroused by the sound of a horse's hoofs clattering in the yard. He wondered sleepily whether this was an early departure or some belated arrival, and then, turning over, managed to lose consciousness for an hour or two longer.

At last, when further sleep had become impossible, he sat up, struck a match, and looking at his watch, discovered that it was nearly six o'clock. He threw his blankets over his arm, stepped over the sprawling limbs of the sleepers, and went out to the stable where he watered his horse, afterward kicking his heels about the place until, in the first glimpse of the dawn, the squaw came shuffling into the kitchen.

Lee went in. 'Get me a cup of coffee and a piece of bread,' he said, putting a fifty-cent piece into her hand. 'That'll be enough for me. I've got to be moving.' The woman filled the kettle from a pail of water on the kitchen table. Lee asked, 'You know that woman who came last night?'

'No, don't know her,' the squaw replied as she set the kettle on the stove.

'Don't know what time she's leaving, I suppose?'

'She's gone. Went at four o'clock.'

Lee whistled softly. That was her horse that he had heard, then. She was losing no time, whatever her business and destination might be. Lee fidgeted while the coffee came to the boil, and had just gulped down a cupful and taken a few bites at the bread and butter which the woman gave him when the landlord came sleepily in, and Lee took the opportunity of settling his bill.

'Well, you're sure off early,' grumbled the proprietor. 'Say, she beat you to it, though!'

'Who is she?' Lee inquired.

'Blamed if I know. Nobody hereabouts seems to know her. But shucks, Little Falls ain't more'n three or four year old! Guess she's the gal of one of the old-timers, back from school or college. Or she'll be goin' up to the Moravian mission, like as not. Yes, sir, that sure must be it. She wouldn't be goin' to any of them hooch runners up to Siston Lake.'

'That's Rathway's joint, isn't it?'

'So they say.' A cunning look came into his eyes. 'I guess we ain't botherin' our heads none about that Free Trader outfit since they're there to stay. No, sir, it don't do to know too much about Captain Carcajou, now that the police is in with him.'

Lee almost betrayed himself as he

struggled not to display his indignation. 'You mean the R.C.M.P.'s been bought by that scum in Montreal?' he demanded.

'That's what they're sayin' in these here parts. See here, stranger, if that ain't so, why don't they get after that Captain Carcajou as they calls him? You heard what he did to that camp of Indians last summer? Sure! Well, I ain't sayin' nothin' and I ain't speakin' for myself, you understand. I'm only sayin' what other folks say. Why, there's two of Rathway's gang in this here hotel.'

'You mean Pierre Cauchon and the red-headed man?'

'Sure I do.' The landlord winked at him. 'Hooch-runners from Siston Lake.'

'What're they doing here?' asked Lee.

'I guess they ain't here for no good. That's why I was wishin' you'd had the sand to stand up to 'em last night, boy!'

3

An Unwelcome Guardian

Lee rode off hot with indignation at the landlord's innuendo about the R.C.M.P. But this soon yielded to anxiety about the woman. The disclosure that the two men were from Siston Lake, and the recollection of the conversation he had overheard, convinced him that they were planning to kidnap and convey her there. Such a plan would seem inconceivable, but Lee knew that the gang, believing their organization firmly entrenched in power, would stop at very little.

However, Lee began to breathe more freely when he had left the squalid little town behind him. He walked or trotted his horse till noon, gradually ascending toward the outskirts of the range through a fairly open country.

The snows might hold off for two or three weeks. Lee felt confident that well within that period he would be able to bring back Pelly, if the latter were in the region, unless he took alarm. In which event, of course, Lee would have to bring his horse back to Little Falls and prepare for a long winter's chase. The new dominion force carried on the tradition of the old Northwest; it did not return without its man.

Siston Lake was admirably adapted for the needs of the Free Traders. It was at the extreme northern limits of the range, or a little beyond, and the head of a lake and river system by which communication could be had by water north to Fort Churchill or York Factory or west as far as Lake Athabasca. The York boat, laden to the gunwale with supplies of liquor, could push anywhere along the thousands of lakes and streams, acting as mother boat in turn to the canoe, with one or more cases. And over all this vast ill-defined district, the hooch-runner had almost unlimited sway, proving a serious rival to the legitimate trading interests, since he carried his poison into the Indian's camping grounds and took his pick of the choicest furs.

His trade embraced a viler one. All along the fringe of white settlement, it was active. It had sprung up like a fungus overnight, during the disorganization of the police in consequence of the war and the readjustment. The gang were steadily embittering the relations between whites and reds, which had been amicable almost since the advent of the first pioneer.

Whichever district the woman was bound for, it was impossible to mistake the course that she would take initially. In front of Lee lay a long backbone of mountain, with only a single pass into the interior over a range of many miles. Scanning the valley carefully, Lee saw, about a mile beyond the pass, a thin curl of smoke rising into the still air.

Satisfied that he had the woman in sight, he hesitated for a while, undecided whether to ride up to her or to camp where he was, keeping a lookout for Pierre and Shorty. In the end he decided that the better course would be to make himself known, and accordingly he descended the slope and followed the trail along the bank of the river until he reached the camp.

The woman had already set up her tent, her horse was tethered near the stream, and she was cooking her dinner at a fire which she had made. She looked very trim and business-like with her sleeves rolled up to her elbows and her air of being completely at home in these surroundings.

As Lee jumped from his horse, she started, then looked at him with an expression of calm which was an attempt to conceal a very obvious trepidation.

'Good evening,' he called. 'I'm travelling your way, and saw your campfire, so took the liberty of joining you, if there's no objection.'

She stared hard at him, as if his advent were some long expected blow that had suddenly fallen. For a few moments, she seemed under the influence of an all-possessing fear. Then mastering it, she answered with the same affectation of indifference: 'You can camp where you like, of course. The range is free for all.'

Lee, a little staggered at the unwilling-ness of this invitation, decided that it would be better for the present not to alarm her with any explanations and proceeded to pitch his tent near hers. While he was unloading his pack and watering his horse, the woman went on with her meal without paying any attention to him.

Lee, feeling both uncomfortable and foolish, was beginning to wish he had waited, when a horse neighed close at hand, his horse and the woman's answered, and a minute later Pierre Cauchon and his companion Shorty rode into view through the gathering darkness.

Pierre's behavior at the sight of Lee was almost ludicrous. He pulled his horse up short with an oath and sat looking from Lee to the woman in almost comical surprise. Shorty, dismounting in a hurried manner, repeated his companion's ges-tures. For several moments, the light of the campfire silhouetted the calm faces of the woman and Lee and the vindictive, scowling ones of the two men.

Then Pierre leaped to the ground. 'By

God, it's the feller that told me 'that'll be all'!' he shouted. 'What you think you're doing here, you damn four-flusher?'

'Maybe the same as you,' said Lee.

'Ho, ho, that's good!' roared the other. 'You think we take you in as pardner, heh?'

'Wouldn't go with you. I've got my own hand to play.'

'You won't play it here, then!' bellowed Shorty. Oaths poured from his lips.

'Pack and vamoose!' yelled Pierre.

Lee held up his hand as the fists threatened him. 'Didn't I tell you I don't fight?' he drawled deceptively.

'You don' fight? By God, you're goin' to fight this time or git!' yelled Pierre. 'You 'fraid of gettin' whipped, eh?'

'That's about the size of it,' laughed Lee. 'That's why I shoot instead — quick and straight and sure, gentlemen!'

His right hand made a movement in his coat pocket, but his automatic was in the holster at the back of his hip, and there was nothing in the pocket more lethal than his pipe.

But Pierre, who was nearest, changed

color. The man was a cur at heart, as Lee had suspected. He leaped back with a snarl. Shorty stepped back, too, though not quite so violently; and the two, withdrawing out of range, proceeded to hold a whispered colloquy, at the end of which, turning away without another word to Lee, they proceeded to set up their camp at a little distance.

Lee turned to the woman, who had stood a silent spectator of the scene. 'I ought to have explained, perhaps,' he said. 'You recognized that man who insulted you last night. A little later I happened to overhear the pair of them speaking of a plan they had formed for intercepting you tonight. I didn't want to alarm you, in case they failed to appear, but that's why I proposed to camp beside you. I think they're unscrupulous customers, and you've probably reached the same decision after the scene that just took place.'

'Thank you, but I assure you that I'm quite capable of protecting myself,' answered the woman, and Lee saw her fingers stray toward a service-size revolver holster at her belt.

'Of course, and I don't want to intrude,' said Lee. 'But as long as these men are here, I think I ought to remain.'

She took a step or two toward him, looking at him fixedly. 'Who and what are you?' she demanded with quivering lips. 'How am I to know that you're not those men's friend, that this isn't all part of an arranged plan?'

'I'm not a friend or associate of those men,' answered Lee indignantly. 'I never saw either of them until one of them insulted you in the hotel yesterday evening. I know that they're planning to do you some harm.'

'Well, and — you?' she asked, trying to keep her voice steady.

'You suspect me?'

'I don't know. I trust nobody. I ask you why you're here.'

'My object in camping here beside you tonight is simply to protect you,' Lee equivocated.

She answered, with an effort at irony, 'And my answer to you is that I don't need protection, but that this country is free for all — for those men and for you.'

She went back into her tent, leaving Lee stupefied. The pair were already seated in front of their fire, munching slabs of bread and raw bacon. They had been watching Lee and the woman furtively throughout the interview. Lee wondered whether the woman's demeanor had given them any inkling of its termination.

If they persuaded her that they were more to be trusted, the situation would be a serious one for her. Lee's position was certainly far more embarrassing than he had anticipated. It was almost as if the woman had decided to throw in her lot with the pair of Free Trader agents. He had not succeeded in convincing her that their motives were evil, perhaps because he had not ventured to voice his real suspicions about them to her. And he had only succeeded in arousing her hostility.

And, looking at the matter in a common-sense light, Lee realized that he had acted wrongly. He should have warned her on his first arrival. He could not blame her for refusing to accept his word. But what was at the bottom of her evident fear of him? The only thing left for him to do was to try to protect her in spite of herself.

The friendly forest had suddenly grown hateful and alien. And then Lee knew what the trouble was. It was the submerged memories of Estelle. She meant nothing to him now, less than nothing, and yet — well, that had been years ago, and he had gone through all that. Still, the imprint was there . . .

Suddenly, as on the night before, he was startled by the low sound of voices. Peering across the grass, he could just distinguish the shadowy outlines of two figures against the men's fire. Very deliberately, Lee drew his automatic from his belt. He had no doubt that Pierre and Shorty were planning mischief; most probably they meant to attack him as a preliminary to overpowering the woman. And as he lay watching them and grimly waiting for their stealthy onset, he felt more than a match for the pair of them.

Minutes went by, however. The pair

seemed an unconscionable time making their arrangements, and all the while the discussion, which was just audible without being intelligible, went on. Lee wondered how long he had been lying there. It was too dark to see his watch. He wondered why they had not waited till morning, when there would be a better chance of taking him unawares.

At last the black shadows separated. One of them was coming toward him with stealthy footsteps. Lee guessed that it was Shorty, the more courageous of the two.

The figure came slowly on. Lee aimed the automatic, his finger steadying on the trigger. He would fire as soon as it made the first hostile movement, as soon as it raised its weapon to cover him.

And then, in amazement, he let the muzzle of his automatic drop. For the figure was not coming toward him, it was going toward the woman's tent.

And it was the woman herself!

Had she then some secret understanding with the two ruffians, and had the episode of the evening at that hotel been a performance staged for some particular purpose? That might almost have appeared credible, but for the conversation that Lee had overheard beside the stove. In the light of that, Lee had to dismiss his surmise.

The only possible explanation at which he could arrive was that the woman had gone to the confederates with his own story, had taxed them, and, of course had been persuaded that his tale was false. Probably they had convinced her that they were friends, and that he had designs upon her.

Mystified and humiliated, Lee went to sleep at last with his ears attuned for any unexpected sound or movement and the automatic within his immediate grasp. Long practice with prisoners whom he had brought single-handed out of the wilds had given him the faculty of sleeping in as complete watchfulness as a wild animal; no enemy could surprise him while he dozed.

But there was no need for these precautions, for nothing disturbed him; and it was the sun, blinking on the edge of the horizon, that awakened him the next morning.

The woman was already cooking her breakfast outside her tent when he emerged, and she returned his salutation with a stiff little bow, keeping her face averted.

Lee attended to his horse and then prepared his breakfast. He had finished before Pierre and Shorty came on the scene. They looked as if they had been drinking heavily the night before, but they made no movement toward either him or the woman until the horses were loaded and ready to start, the woman briefly declining Lee's assistance and handling her own gear like an expert.

Then Shorty came up to Lee.

'See here, what's the great idea?' he asked in a tone that was meant to be conciliatory. 'My pardner and me was wonderin' if we couldn't fix up this little misunderstandin'. I guess you're barkin' up the wrong tree, ain't you?'

'Meaning?'

'Meanin' as how my pardner and me don't mean no harm to this young lady.

We're on a prospectin' trip, and we don't want no outsiders buttin' in on our property.'

'How about this lady?'

'Now, pardner, you got things sized up wrong, I tell you. If she's goin' our way, why, we ain't going to pretend not to see each other. Now I dunno where you're bound for, and I don't care, but I give you the best tip you ever had, since you say you don't like trouble. There ain't no gold in Stony Range, and the best thing you can do is to beat it back to Little Falls. That's about it.'

'If there's no gold in Stony Range, why are you prospecting here?'

'Say,' shouted Shorty, 'I guess my pardner and me knows our business without no outsider buttin' in. I've put the cards face up on the table. Now how about it?'

'Nothing doing.'

Shorty glared at him. 'Say, what kinda game are you playin'? That's what we want to know,' he demanded. 'Is this a showdown or ain't it?'

'Not for me,' answered Lee.

'All right!' Shorty clambered on his horse with an oath and cantered back to where Pierre was standing, cursing as he tried to tighten his girth. A colloquy ensued. The pair rode up to the woman, who was already in her saddle. There followed an animated pantomime, with gesticulations toward Lee. The woman seemed to sit obstinately mute, as if she remained neutral.

Suddenly Shorty wheeled his horse about. 'Come 'long. Pierre, I guess we've give the fool his chance!' he shouted. And, to Lee's surprise, the pair kicked their mounts in the ribs, and in a moment were off at full gallop, along the trail leading into the range beyond the valley.

The woman and Lee looked after them till they were out of sight. Then she rode slowly up to where Lee was sitting on his mount.

'I understand that you insist on accompanying me?' she asked. 'Despite the fact that I have made it clear I don't require your company?'

'I'm sorry you take my presence in that spirit. I assure you I have no desire to be troublesome, but under the circumstances I must ask leave to go with you as far as your destination.'

She bit her lip. 'I suppose you mean what you're doing is a kindness,' she said. 'And since you appear determined to accompany me, I suppose there's no use in our sulking with each other, is there?'

'I wish we could be friends,' answered Lee, offering her his hand.

But the woman's little hand did not advance to meet his. 'I mean,' she said, 'if we are companions, we may as well acknowledge it, though I assure you I'm a very unwilling one. That doesn't imply friendliness. I hope your persistence will be properly rewarded.'

'Let me say once and for all,' Lee answered, 'that I have no desire to pry into your business. I don't even know your name, or wish to ask it.'

'If I dared to let myself believe that you have no other purpose in view than just to protect me — ' she began. 'But it's impossible. Men aren't like that. They're wolves, they're wolverines, treacherous, cunning; remorseless. Oh, if I could believe you — '

'I'd do anything on earth to help you,' answered Lee. 'If you mean seriously that you find it so difficult to make your decision between those men and myself — a man is said to bear the stamp of his life and character on his face. I don't know what impression I give to others, but I know what impression those two men gave me. Can't you read their faces? If you can't trust me, can you at least say honestly that you trust them?'

She looked at him fearfully. 'If it were simply a matter of choosing between yourself and them, I should put my trust in you without the smallest hesitation. But — oh, I can't say any more. It's hopeless — it's worse degradation than death to me, and yet I must keep up my strength and resolution — I must — '

The breakdown came upon her like a lightning stroke. She seemed to crumple up; she sobbed desolately into her hands.

Lee moved to her side. 'Do you know,' he said, 'we have to trust people in this life, even if they deceive us. It doesn't harm us to be betrayed.' But he was thinking of Estelle as he spoke, and he wondered how far that was true. Estelle's betrayal had changed the whole setting of his life for him. 'Trust me,' he said. 'Let me help you. Tell me where you're going, and why, and what those men are to you.'

It was a full half-minute before she took her hands from her face, but she did not reply. All that day they rode together. But not until they had pitched their tents again for the night did she refer to the men who had threatened her.

'Will you be frank with me?' she asked. 'Will you tell me what you're doing in the range?'

'I'm not free to do so.'

'And am I free? Is any one of us free?' she cried. 'No, it's impossible. I must just go on and ask God to give me strength to bear it! Don't speak to me for a few moments — there. I'm sorry I made such a fool of myself!' She smiled. 'And if you insist on riding with me — well, I can't help it. Only, I warn you, you're going into danger — grave danger. Those two men — I'm afraid they may be planning to do you some injury.'

'I don't think they're likely to try very hard,' answered Lee.

'But — but others — ' she whispered. 'It's not just them! You begged me to trust you. You said that you would do anything to help me. Did you mean that?'

'Anything that's possible. If it lies in my power.'

'Then would you — would you kill a man for me? A human wolf, one of those devil creatures that doesn't deserve to live? Would you kill him to help me? Wait before you answer. He's a man who has betrayed those who have trusted him, made humanity a mockery; he's the foulest thing that creeps upon the earth. Earth should be rid of him. If I help you, will you shoot him down like the savage dog that he is, in cold blood, without danger to yourself, while he's sleeping? If I help you?'

'No,' answered Lee quietly.

She laughed in mocking scorn. 'So I supposed,' she answered. 'You men, with your professions of loyalty and service

— you're all the same when it comes to the test.'

'I won't commit murder in cold blood and without provocation.'

'No, of course not. You see, there might be just a little danger in it. He's very crafty, and your offer of help didn't include personal risk.'

Lee's fingers closed on her arm. 'That's not the way,' he said. 'One doesn't right wrongs with wrongs, or even up scores by murder. Tell me everything, and I pledge myself to see that whatever wrong you've suffered shall be redressed.'

'Oh, I've heard that before, and when I put you to the test I found just what those words were worth,' she answered lightly. 'No, please forget what I've just said to you. There's no such man as I spoke of. There couldn't be, for he would have been killed long ago. I was just wondering whether I was to take you seriously or not — and I found we were both playing a game. Good night!'

She moved away abruptly and went into her tent.

And all that night he lay, hardly dozing,

44

his automatic beside his hand, waiting and wondering.

4

The Trap is Sprung

In the morning, she greeted him with a forced gaiety. She nodded and smiled when she came out of her tent.

'Well, we shall ride on together today, I suppose,' she said. 'I've told you that I don't desire your company, and that your enterprise is probably a dangerous one. You've taken the responsibility upon yourself, with the understanding that we go as companions instead of enemies. Is that not so?'

And this time, it was the woman who extended her hand. Lee took it and held it for a moment in his own. 'That's the understanding,' he answered. 'I intend to see you to your destination, wherever that is, and after that you need not be afraid of my troubling you anymore.'

'And as for yesterday,' said the woman, 'you will forget that I was a little hysterical and upset? You see, it's quite an ordeal, going on so long a journey, and I was tired and said foolish things that had no meaning in them at all.' She watched Lee's face closely as she said this, but Lee did not reply.

They mounted and continued the journey. It was about ten o'clock when they heard two or three full reverberations in the distance. The woman, who was riding a few yards ahead of Lee, reined in and stood her horse upon a turfy hillock, waiting for him to catch up with her.

'What was that?' she asked, looking at him with startled eyes.

'Dynamite,' Lee responded.

'Dynamite? Why — who would — ?'

'Some prospector blasting rock on his claim, no doubt,' answered Lee, and again there sounded a detonation.

'It rather startled me,' she said. 'I've been afraid since those two men left us — afraid some harm might come to you from them. You'll be on your guard, won't you?'

'Yes, I promise you that,' Lee answered; and she fixed her eyes on his face with her peculiar scrutiny for a few moments, and then urged her horse onward.

The afternoon began to wear away. They were slowly descending toward the northern pass of the range, beyond which lay the immense territories that they had seen. They began to traverse precarious defiles, overhung by huge boulders, prismatic from the corrosion of the season. Underneath them, at the bottom of a long decent, in places nearly perpendicular, the torrent raced among the rocks. It was so still upon those heights that the rush of the torrent far underneath them sounded thunderous; and the air was so calm, the sky so blue, that it might have been an Italian summer rather than Canadian autumn. An eagle floating motionless high overhead seemed to have been pinned against the background of the blue void.

The woman reined in and waited for Lee to ride up to her. 'Be very careful with that horse of yours,' he said. 'There's a difficult bit a little distance ahead, but it's the last, and then we'll have an easy journey down through the pass.'

She started off again, Lee following some twenty paces behind her; but suddenly Lee's horse balked, laid back his ears and snorted, planted his forefeet firmly and refused to move.

It was almost impossible to dismount and lead him, for at that point, the narrowest part of the trail, there was hardly standing room for man and beast together. Lee held in the animal with a tight rein and patted his quivering flanks. He could not understand what had alarmed it, but now some instinct, perhaps communicated from the beast's brain to his, seemed to tell of danger threatening.

He glanced at the woman, and saw that she was almost across the danger zone. He dared not call to her, for fear of startling her. And indeed there was no reason to call, although that baseless instinct was now becoming so strong that it almost amounted to conviction.

He could not see the least cause for apprehension anywhere. His fears appeared absurd; and yet that electric message of warning went flashing back and forth between his mind and that of his frightened mount.

Then suddenly there came the roar of an explosion, muffled underground; the next moment an enormous crack appeared in the face of the wall of solid rock overhead, which trembled and appeared to move toward him, as if pushed by a gigantic hand. Before the reverberations had died away, Lee heard a faint crepitating sound, like the rustling of paper — the sliding of the interior strata, one upon another.

A little avalanche of stones dislodged from the surface and came rushing down the face of the cliff midway between the woman and himself. Had Lee's horse not stopped, it would have been swept over the edge of the precipice. Another roar, and a huge rock toppled and fell, this time behind, and smashed into a score of fragments which went rolling into the chasm below, waking a hundred reverberations among the hills.

And with that, Lee understood the devilish scheme that was in the working. The dynamiting which he had heard that afternoon was the preliminary work of the two men in preparing their trap; now they had set fuses among the rocks at the narrowest point of the trail, with the purpose of blowing him to destruction. And it was a murder plan that would leave no evidence behind it, surer and safer than a rifle shot.

Another explosion; and between the sound of the dull roar and the upheaval, Lee, seeing the woman apparently trying to urge her plunging animal back toward him, stood up in his stirrups and waved his hand frantically toward her.

'Go back! Go back!' he shouted.

But the woman seemed bewildered; she only clung to her plunging, snorting beast, over which she had lost control, while it pawed the air and danced desperately upon the narrow way.

Lee vaulted from his horse, struggled upon the edge of the precipice, regained his footing, and ran toward her. He caught at her horse's bridle. 'Jump! Jump!' he shouted, holding out his arms.

And the few following seconds seemed to extend through all eternity. Another roar, and the whole face of the mountain wall appeared to crumple into a landslide. As in a helpless dream, Lee saw the falling wall strike the woman's horse in the flank and send it screaming into the chasm. And, as he vainly grasped at her, an impact shot him over the precipice as if he had been hurled from the mouth of a cannon.

He felt himself hurtling into space; he grasped at emptiness and went tumbling far down into unconsciousness.

5

The Severed Strands

The returning scene of consciousness was at first only the dim knowledge of pain, in terms of which Lee visualized existence. That pain seemed to have existed for eternity, filling all space and time. It usurped all the functions of the body. He was the nucleus of it, sprawling like an inert being at the heart of creation, and out of him pain radiated through the universe.

And then came sight — chaos of brown and green, fantastic mountains clothed with sparse unbranching trees, earth's primitive creation, huge continents that he bestrode, a Brobdingnag of his species, solitary in the world.

Lee became aware that his eyes were open. And very slowly he grew aware of his own identity. He began looking about him.

Then he made the discovery that the mountains he had seen were boulders; the vegetation, moss and grasses. He was lying upon the ground with a great rock on either side of him, halfway down the gorge at the bottom of which the torrent coursed. Low scrub alder and other growth formed a sort of fanwork over him, completely concealing him. Above this fanwork was a glimpse of the gray sky.

He began to remember things. He had been riding, had been thrown from his mount. The inspector had sent him to bring somebody in — Snell, Kelly — Pelly! He must have encountered Pelly and have been shot. Pelly had been a fool not to finish the job. He must get after him again. And what had happened to his horse?

Now from where he lay, he had a glimpse of the fawn flanks, the shining steel circlets beneath the hoofs. His horse was lying lower down the slope, at the very edge of the rocks beside the torrent. Pelly must have shot his horse as well. Or perhaps it was only the horse, and Lee had been stunned by the fall.

The red rim of the sun was just dipping into the horizon, and Lee remembered that when he had last seen it, it was midway in the western sky. But he had seen it from a cliff top.

With that, the woman flashed into the picture. Lee saw her and her horse toppling down the ravine. He remembered his own fall, the landslide, the dynamite. Memory grew complete, and the last links snapped into place.

He realized that he had been flung from the heights above, and that by a miracle of luck his descent into the rock-strewn torrent had been arrested by the scrub growth which held him. Otherwise, those rocks would have ground and battered him almost out of semblance to a man, or tossed him into the whirling torrent. As it was, it was a miracle that he had survived the fall. Probably he was badly injured. He must count on broken limbs.

He tried to rise, and instantly his body screamed its protest. With immense difficulty, he succeeded in getting upon his hands and knees. He flexed each of his limbs in turn. He felt his body and ribs; he patted himself all over.

It was incredible, but though every muscle in his body seemed twisted, and he was aching and bruised from head to foot, no bones appeared to be broken. Peering along the edge of the ravine, Lee saw the woman's horse lying a little distance away.

The effort to get upon his feet seemed to consume an incredible period of time. By the exercise of all his will, Lee managed to keep his balance until the rocking earth had grown comparatively stable. Then, forcing his rebellious limbs and muscles into coordination, he staggered toward the woman's horse.

It was alive, but its back and limbs were broken, so that it was completely paralyzed. It looked at Lee as he approached out of its bright, pathetic eyes, instinct with the foreknowledge of death.

Lee was sick with the fear that he would either find the woman dead, battered almost out of recognition among the rocks, or missing; drowned in the torrent below. He searched every inch of the surrounding terrain within a radius of three hundred yards, and then abandoned hope. Anger, boiling up within him, assisted in reviving strength. He would follow her murderers and shoot them down like the wild beasts they were.

Before leaving the side of the injured horse, Lee drew his automatic, which had remained buckled in his belt holster throughout the fall, and mercifully ended the animal's life with a single shot over the heart.

Now there remained the pursuit, and vengeance; then the original duty of picking up Pelly. But he swore that he would take one man, not three, to Manistree. And with that decision, he retraced his steps, until once more he stood beside the gorge between the dead horses.

The contents of the packs had burst from the broken canvas and lay scattered everywhere, but the rifle was not to be found. Two or three cartridges at the edge of the chasm were all he discovered.

He turned doggedly to take up the pursuit again. But as he was passing the woman's horse, something yellow and shining on the ground caught his eye. He stooped to examine it. Long tresses of pale yellow-brown hair coiled round his fingers. It was the hair of the woman!

He tried to pick it up, but the ends were pinned under the dead animal, probably caught in the broken girth. The ends that lay upon the ground appeared to have been roughly severed with a knife. There was no doubt it was the woman's hair, and the tresses must have been severed within a few inches of her head, for there was more than three feet of them in view, trailing along the ground.

He tugged at them to detach them, but it was a matter of considerable effort, and he only succeeded in releasing them strand by strand. At last, however, he managed to detach them, and, after a moment's hesitation, he thrust them into the bosom of his shirt.

And then of a sudden he understood what had happened, and his heart gave a bound. The woman had not been flung into the water. She must somehow have become pinned by the hair beneath her horse after her fall; it had come near rolling on her, and her hair had been cut off to affect her quick release.

She was not dead. She had been carried off by the two ruffians.

It was nearly dark when Lee crossed the pass a second time. And he went on, under the light of the moon, scanning the trail ahead of him and the riverbank for the kidnapers' encampment. But hours went by and he did not come upon it; and only the dark river, with its twisted, desolate banks, and the eternal forest, disclosed themselves.

In the small hours the wind veered, bringing with it a storm of icy pelting rain which changed to a driving sleet. The whistling pellets stung and whipped his face, and all through the storm Lee continued to struggle onward.

It was a superb exhibition of the force of will. Hour after hour he went on, until, in the beginning of that hour before the dawn when everything grows still, when the first faintness of the dawn begins to mingle with the darkness, he became conscious that the river had widened into a lake, one arm of which, thrust out before him, barred his course. On either side of this lake, the forests had given place to reedy swamp.

And, lifting up his eyes, he saw upon a low elevation in front of him the log huts of the Free Traders' camp. Then he knew that the long chase had come to an end.

And with that, Lee shook the fatigue from him, knowing that he must hold on to all his strength and wit for an hour or two longer, and that what he had to do he must do quickly, craftily, boldly.

He did not know how many men were in the Free Traders' headquarters, but he must save the woman; get her away.

The arm of the lake that was thrust out between the elevation and the end of the trail was no more than two hundred yards, if as much, in width. Satisfying himself that there was no way of approach except by water unless there existed some trail across the swamps, which there was no time to find, Lee waded into the lake, then swam.

The current ran strong; the shock of the icy water at first numbed, then invigorated him. It cleared the doubts and fears of night from his limbs. Swimming diagonally against the current, in a few minutes Lee had reached the flat terrain at the base of the promontory.

He waded ashore, shaking himself like a dog. On the terrain were heaped great mounds of waste and garbage from the encampment above; piles of disintegrating cans, rotting cases, innumerable bottles partly covered with the silt and protruding from it the accumulation of a long period.

Looking through the mist, Lee perceived a small York boat of the kind used universally between Hudson's Bay and the Mackenzie, riding moored against the rocky edge of the promontory some distance away.

The elevation, long, low, and flat, formed an ideal fortress; with the only approach apparently by water, it was evident that it would be a formidable proposition for anybody of the police to attack in the event of defense.

Lee began to make his way across the terrain, keeping under the shelter of the cliff to escape observation from the huts above. It was growing light now, and he could see the surroundings clearly. He reached the end of the patch of ground without coming upon any place by which it might be possible to ascend to the summit of the promontory.

He hurried back, doubling on his tracks, examining the cliff in the other direction. He reached the other side of the flat terrain only to find that the elevation presented the same insurmountable flank to him everywhere.

But then of a sudden he realized that the York boat must be drawn up at the point of entrance. And it was with this that he must make his flight with the woman, beaching the boat across the water somewhere; taking to the forests.

Without hesitation, he took to the water again and swam with steady strokes toward it. In two or three minutes he had gained its side. The kidnapers must have left their horses at some refuge or rendezvous in the forest and brought the woman by boat to Siston Lake. And it was evident that they could not have arrived so much as an hour before.

The York boat was moored opposite a cleft in the great dome of the promontory, which offered easy access to the summit. Lee waded ashore once more, but before attempting the ascent, he drew his automatic from its holster and examined it. The holster had a waterproof lining, and only a few drops glistened upon the surface of the weapon.

Scrambling up the acclivity, Lee saw the two huts among the trees immediately overhead. He scrambled up the low wall of rocks, and was about to step on to the elevation when all of a sudden a man came out of the farther hut and made his way toward the nearer one.

Lee ducked his head down just in time to escape detection, and through the interstices between the boulders he watched the man until he had entered the hut immediately above him. He looked about forty years of age. He was shorter than Lee, but apparently of great strength. He had an untrimmed black beard, he walked with hunched shoulders, and there was a look of singular ferocity and cunning on his face.

A dangerous, treacherous customer, Lee thought. *Rathway!*

When he had disappeared within the hut, Lee stood up. Craning over the rocks, he could just catch a glimpse of the interior. He saw the man standing over what looked like a camp bed, on which he could distinguish the head and shoulders of a woman lying perfectly still.

Lee's heart leaped. He gripped his automatic and levelled it. A single shot from where he stood, well-aimed, would be sufficient.

And at that moment, instinct and desire struggled with discipline as never before, with the maxim inculcated during his eight years of service never to take life except when life was in immediate danger.

Then discipline won. Lee let the muzzle drop.

At that moment, he heard the growling voice of the man and the answer of a third person inside the hut — a woman. The words were inaudible, and now, hesitating no longer, Lee scrambled over the rocky ridge and made his way toward the door obliquely, so as to remain concealed from the sight of those within.

The man's voice rose in a falsetto snarl. 'What do I mean to do with her? What would I do with her! She's mine, ain't she?'

'And what about me?' Low as the voice was, restrained yet passionate, something about it sent a sudden shiver through Lee, and for a few moments he could only remain a helpless listener.

'You?' he laughed. 'You can stay on here as long as you want to, I guess. There's Pierre and Shorty, if you want a man — '

'You coward!' Her voice was vibrant with indignation. 'I tell you you've made a mistake in bringing that woman here. You'll regret it. That mine doesn't exist. And when she finds you've fooled her, what are you going to do?'

'So we're jealous, are we? Well, I've been tired of you for a long time,' he jeered.

'Jim — ' There was desperate pleading in the woman's tones. 'I gave up all for you. Let her go. Don't cast me off. I love you, Jim.'

And now Lee knew. A mist trembled before his eyes, and, gripping his automatic, he sprang forward to the door. He must have shouted, though he was unconscious of everything but the desire to get Rathway by the throat.

Wheeling, Rathway swore, and then, heedless of Lee's pistol, leaped. But in the moment before they closed, Lee saw the woman's face and knew her for his dead love, who had broken his life and changed it utterly — Estelle.

Lee did not shoot. Instinctively he obeyed that unwritten law of the police tradition not to take life save in the last extremity.

But the sight of this sinister figure, the wholly incredible presence there of Estelle, the woman who had wrecked his life, and the woman lying unconscious on the bed in this man's power, aroused in Lee's heart a sleeping devil of whose existence he had hardly been aware at any time in his life before.

He was conscious only of a mad desire to kill, but to kill with nature's own weapons, in obedience to man's instinctive law.

Clubbing his automatic, Lee leaped to meet Rathway's charge, and breast to breast they met, rebounding like balls of rubber. Rathway's hand shot out and grasped Lee's wrist before the weapon descended. Then, interlocked, they stood almost motionless, matched so evenly that neither budged an inch before the other for a full minute.

Rathway's sneering face was upturned to Lee's. Malice and hate gleamed from his bloodshot eyes. Beside them stood Estelle, with her hands still clasped in the gesture that she had made at the moment of Lee's intervention, struck dumb and motionless with terror and amazement.

Rathway was proving himself the stronger. Malice and hate became triumph, derision. Lee's pistol hand was being bent back. Lee adapted himself with quick instinct to the discovery that he was the weaker in arm and shoulder muscles. As Rathway's body slowly assumed a forward tilt, shifting his center of gravity, Lee suddenly drove his knee into the back of Rathway, causing the man to stumble forward. The impetus of the body projected against him sent the pistol flying out of Lee's hand; but Lee, in the moment of Rathway's loss of equipoise, drove his fist home into his face, splitting his lips and sending him reeling.

In an instant they were together again, delivering and receiving a succession of pile-driver blows that fell like flails upon each other's faces and bodies. They clinched, rebounded, clinched again; then suddenly Rathway got home a furious kick to the groin that sent Lee stumbling.

For the first time Estelle screamed, and that aroused Lee to the consciousness that he must finish his enemy almost immediately, before aid arrived. He shook away the film that was creeping over his eyes, and, sick and nauseated from the kick, he closed with Rathway again. They went to the floor of the hut together, and struggled there like two dogs in the dirt.

There was no longer any attempt at fisticuffs. The primitive instinct to rend and tear possessed both of them equally. They scrambled about the floor of the hut, clawing at each other's throats. Lee got Rathway's beard in his right hand, and with his left began smashing at his nose and lips.

Rathway bellowed, and his hands closed on Lee's throat, clinging there, worrying him like a bulldog. Lee felt that he was fainting. He was slowly forced over; Rathway's fingers closed on his neck.

The two tightened, and the walls of the hut began to waver. Lee's trachea flattened; his lungs felt as if they would burst. Rathway grinned diabolically into his face, his beard like some foul fungus. Lee flung his arms out instinctively to breathe. One of his hands encountered something. It was the pistol.

Lee's fingers closed on it. And, as if he concentrated all that was left of himself in his left hand, he raised the weapon and brought it crashing down upon Rathway's skull.

Instantly Rathway's clutch relaxed, his eyes glazed, as chicken's eyes glaze at the moment of death. The man's head dropped foolishly forward on Lee's breast. A stream of curses was cut off in foolish mutterings.

Lee struggled to his feet and stood gasping for breath, while Rathway, mumbling stupidly, swayed to and fro upon his knees on the floor of the hut.

Suddenly Estelle appeared to be galvanized into life. With a low cry she ran to Rathway's side, knelt down by him, and put her arms about him. She drew his head down on her knees and began chafing his hands. She looked at Lee in bitter hate.

'Haven't you done me wrong enough in the past, that you should come here to kill my man?' she cried. 'Do you think you can arrest him? You couldn't get a mile from here before you'd be captured.'

But Lee, without paying any attention to her, hurried to the bedside and looked down at the captured woman. She lay there, an unconscious huddled heap, one knee bent under her. Her face was deathly white, and there was a scalp wound at the back of her head which had been bleeding freely. She breathed faintly. Her hair was cut short and jagged about her head, making her look more than ever like a boy.

Estelle laid Rathway gently down and came toward Lee with sudden comprehension. 'It's for *her*?' she whispered earnestly, laying her hand upon his arm. 'You came here to rescue her?' She read the answer in his eyes. 'Oh, I'll help you. *I'll help you*, then!' she cried wildly. 'You'll take her away! Trust me, then, and listen to me. There's no time for explanations now. It's only a miracle of luck you found him alone. Some men are due at any moment in the motorboat. Two more have gone to meet them with a message. They're coming from down the lake. There may be just time to escape them. You must take the York boat. You can't pull it alone against the stream. Keep to the left channel past the island, then run ashore, and you'll be safe in the forest, wherever you're going. Hurry, hurry!'

Lee made no audible reply, but his mind automatically registered Estelle's instructions. He bent over the woman again, raised her in his arms so that her face rested against his shoulder, and carried her out of the hut.

As he turned at the entrance, he saw that Rathway had risen to his knees again. Blood was dripping from the wound in his scalp, and he was staring about him in the eager effort to remember.

Lee crossed the open space at a run, scrambled down the descent, placed the woman in the bottom of the boat, and, seizing a pair of oars, began to pull furiously for midstream. The current caught him and sent him whirling along toward the long, flat, wooded island in the middle of the lake that came into view.

In a minute or two, however, the flow of the river, diffused over the whole of the lake, ceased to afford him any appreciable assistance. The heavy York boat responded only slightly to the pull of the single oarsman, seeming to creep on by inches.

Suddenly Rathway appeared upon the

promontory, Estelle beside him, clinging to him. He pushed her from him, shaking his fist at Lee; and his hoarse, furious bellows came across the water like the roaring of an enraged beast of the forest. For a few moments, he stood thus outlined against the rising sun; then he disappeared.

Lee struggled at the oars. From time to time he strained his ears to catch the sounds of the oncoming motorboat. Although the new arrivals would know nothing of his activities at the promontory, he was pretty sure that any solitary oarsman appearing in that region would be stopped by them; then he would be at their mercy, for Pierre and Shorty would be members of their party.

If once he could round the point of the island, where he would be out of sight both of the promontory and of the motorboat coming up the channel, he could pull straight for the lake shore, take to the woods and make for the mission, where he meant to leave the woman for safekeeping.

Lee felt his spirits rise. It was a matter

only of a half hour. And there were two packs in the boat. With one of these, they could live in the forest till she was able to continue the journey. And, looking down at the unconscious woman, he felt again that odd sense of tender companionship in his heart for her, fed perhaps by the realization that the one thing he had dreaded had not come to pass.

He had feared that if ever again he met Estelle, the old passion for her would flare up in him. Now they had met, and that love of the past filled him only with wonder, and a vast pity for her that she should have come to be the discarded companion of an outlaw. He no longer condemned her. He no longer resented his wrongs. It was as if a cleansing sponge had been passed over all that had happened.

The left channel between the island and the shore was almost blocked in places with reeds and water growth. It was a huge water morass of dead vegetation, nearly half a mile wide. A few more strokes, and he meant to pull toward the lake's shore.

The pulling had grown to be an enormous effort. Lee was again conscious of fatigue. He felt drowsy in the increasing warmth of the sun. He could have fallen asleep in a moment.

But suddenly his senses leaped into activity. From far away he had caught the urgent warning of imminent danger: the faint put-putting of the motorboat.

6

Trapped on the Island

Instantly, Lee began straining at the oars again, redoubling his efforts to gain the shore before the motorboat rounded the point.

Suddenly his attention was attracted by something creeping along the opposite shore. It was a small canoe and a single man in it — Rathway!

It was impossible not to admire the courage that inspired the man after the drubbing he had received. Rathway was, of course, on his way to warn the expected party.

Lee drove hard for the left middle channel of the lake. The main body of Siston Lake came into view, a vast expanse of shining water, the shores receding into the hazy distance, out of which a small black object began to be visible, like a bug skimming the surface.

Now the canoe containing Rathway was almost abreast of him. A few more furious pulls — ten, fifteen; now canoe and motorboat and promontory were all hidden behind the point of the island. Lee labored at the oars, turning the York boat's head toward the bank. Once there, they would be safe. But his strength was failing him. Curse the clumsy boat, which hardly seemed to move!

The putting of the motor engine had grown infernally loud. It added a horror of its own to that sense of pursuit which makes the bravest man something of a coward, the added horror of the fugitive who hears the distant bay of blood-hounds.

Then suddenly the motor stopped. That meant that the canoe had come abreast of it. Rathway was passing the intelligence. And the shore was still a hundred yards distant.

There was no chance of reaching it unobserved. It would be neck and neck for it, and it was doubtful whether Lee could have escaped alone, much less with the woman and the pack to carry. He swung the boat's blunt nose toward the nearest patch of reeds. Twenty yards! He put all his strength into that last effort. Now the reeds were closing about him. In front of him, a little open channel appeared. Using one shortened oar as a paddle, he drove vigorously, and found himself in temporary safety. A thick wall of reeds extended between himself and open water, rendering the York boat invisible.

Then the motor began to roar. The shouts of its occupants became audible. The motorboat had rounded the point. Lee had escaped discovery by the skin of his teeth.

And very cautiously, so as not to betray his whereabouts by any undue agitation of the reeds, Lee pushed the boat toward the island. His plan must now be to drive ashore, trusting to escape detection until nightfall and to make the wooded shore of the lake in the darkness.

Through the reeds the marshy foreshore began to be visible, and a sandy spit projecting to the water's edge. Above it was a hammock overgrown with birch and red spruce, with a tangle of sheep laurel and birch and poplar behind it.

Lee worked his heavy boat noiselessly toward this spit. But suddenly he stopped. The motorboat was coming up the open channel, hardly a stone's throw distant. He could hear Rathway in it, bellowing commands to his companions. He could hear the reeds rustling against the boat's sides as she forced her passage through them.

'They're not in here!' he heard Rathway say with an oath. 'Get into the channel and beat it up to the island.'

Lee, crouching in the stern of the York boat with his pistol in his hand, breathed a sigh of relief as the motorboat withdrew. The roar of her engine began to grow fainter. In a few minutes it had died away.

Lee forced the York boat ashore upon the spit of sand, and stooping, raised the woman in his arms and carried her into the shelter of the spruce thicket, where he laid her gently down. For the first time since her injury he had the opportunity to examine her. Her prolonged unconsciousness alarmed him.

But she was beginning to revive at last, and, after assuring himself that the pulse beat was fairly strong, he proceeded to make as thorough an examination as possible of her injuries. He turned his examination first to the cut in her head. He tore strips from his shirt, went down to the water and cleansed them thoroughly; then, returning, he proceeded to wash and bandage it. It was a bad gash from a rock, and she had bled a great deal, which was a good thing, relieving the concussion which had no doubt been the cause of the prolonged insensitivity. Having ascertained that she seemed to have received no bodily injuries beyond contusions, Lee examined her limbs. He saw that one knee hung awry. In a moment he had her gaiter off, and discovered that the joint had been dislocated.

Short of the setting of a broken bone, there are few operations more painful than the restoration of a joint into position, and Lee prayed fervently that the woman's unconsciousness would last until he had put to her service the knowledge which he had acquired with the Canadian army medical corps upon the western frontier.

It was unnerving, holding that white knee between his hands, so fragile, delicate, so wonderful when viewed as a piece of mechanism which he was to manipulate like some clumsy journeyman called in to repair the work of a master. Fortunately, Lee had assisted at precisely that same operation several times in the field; and, trying to disregard the moans of pain that came from the woman's lips as he proceeded, he fumbled with the displaced bone.

But that struggle was terrible, for the body of itself knows no dignity. Conscious, Lee knew that the woman would neither have flinched nor moaned; but unconscious she could not control the protests of the body, which had to be restrained by something almost brutal in its frank violence.

But Lee struggled on, feeling the shaft head of the bone scour the edges of the socket under the cap. A final struggle, the weight of his whole body and shoulders thrown to his task, and suddenly it was accomplished. The joint slipped into position, the tortured body ceased its protest, and Lee rose, the perspiration streaming down his face.

Trembling in the nervous reaction from the struggle, Lee listened to the increasing noise of the motorboat again. It rose to a roar as it passed again along the channel immediately in front of his hiding place, and gradually dwindled away.

Leaving the woman where she had fallen back into unconsciousness, Lee ascended one of the spruce trees and scanned the channel. The motorboat was moving up the shore of the island along the edge of the reeds. It contained Rathway and two other men.

Another York boat was coming from the direction of the promontory. This contained three men also. Six on the trail; and Lee guessed that they would leave no nook unsearched in their determination to locate himself and the woman.

The island appeared to be about a mile in length by a third wide. Lee, seeing that discovery was only a matter of time, decided that it would be better to abandon the boat and take refuge somewhere in the underbrush. If the York boat had not been found by nightfall, he could return with the woman and try to escape to the mainland. If it were discovered, their situation would be no worse.

He strapped one of the packs about his back, picked up the woman, and, thus encumbered, proceeded through the thick brush, making for the opposite shore, where he put the woman down in a small declivity where the growth was thickest. Removing the tin pannikin from the outside of the pack, he obtained water and poured some down the woman's throat. He noted that the swallowing reflex was present, a favorable sign in unconsciousness, as he had learned at the front.

Toward the middle of the afternoon, the sun, which had shone brilliantly throughout the morning, went permanently behind the clouds. Another snowstorm was brewing up. A few soft flakes began to fall.

Suddenly a distant hubbub broke out and continued. There was no mistaking what was meant. The York boat had been discovered.

The Free Traders began to beat across the island, calling to one another. Their voices gradually sounded nearer. Crouching beside the woman in the thick of the brush, Lee waited. At a distance, he saw two of them pass through the trees and disappear. The shouting died away.

As soon as they had passed him, leaving the woman where she lay, Lee slipped softly through the undergrowth, making his way back to the sandy spit. His expectations were confirmed. The York boat had disappeared.

Re-ascending the spruce tree, he saw the two York boats moored to the motorboat in mid-channel, a man with a rifle seated in it on guard. They were trapped on the island.

Lee made his way back, and waited while the afternoon wore away. The snow fell thicker. He took off his mackinaw and placed it over the woman.

She was no longer in a coma, but

semiconscious, and unaware of her surroundings. She muttered and tossed; sometimes it was all Lee could do to quiet her. And the disjointed fragments of speech that fell from her lips indicated the same mental anguish that she had revealed to him during their ride through the range. He shuddered to think of her sufferings if she had awakened to find herself a prisoner in Rathway's power at the promontory.

And even in the darkness of their desperate situation, he drew new hope from his resolution. And gradually his plans formed in his mind.

Then night began to fall, and Lee breathed a vast sigh of relief. Unless his plans miscarried, they should be safe upon the mainland well before midnight.

These depended, of course, upon his being able to capture one of the boats. The best plan for the Free Traders would have been to have withdrawn them to the promontory, knowing that Lee could not swim with the woman across that stretch of ice-cold water. Lee felt sure that in their eagerness, feeling secure in their numbers, they would encamp upon the shore, either beaching the boats or leaving them anchored under the single guard in the middle channel.

About half an hour after dark, he set out on his investigations. He moved through the brush as softly as any Indian, and, booted though he was, hardly a twig crackled under his feet.

Making his way toward the central portion, where the trees were sparser and the ground undulating, he soon discovered what he was looking for: the distant glow of a campfire. Four men were seated around the fire, drinking and conversing loudly. It was impossible to make out their faces in the darkness, but Lee waited patiently until the light of the fire fell upon each, and ascertained that none of them was bearded. Rathway, then, was either in charge of the motorboat with the sixth man, or had been forced to return to his headquarters, owing to his condition.

Lee circled the camp, and discovered to his joy the York boat beached on the shore about twenty-five yards distant. The men had not troubled to draw it up on birch rollers, where it would have been a matter of time and labor to float it again; it lay with its keel in the mud, careening to the lap of the little waves.

Lee cogitated. If the men got drunk that night, it might be possible to make off with the boat without arousing them. On the other hand, the probabilities were that through fear of Rathway, they would stay sober enough to guard it effectively. And the delay was telling upon his nerves.

He decided that at all costs it was necessary to make the attempt as quickly as possible. He made his way back to the woman, strapped the pack on his back, and, taking her in his arms, began to approach the encampment by a circuitous route through the trees.

In the darkness, staggering over the uneven ground, and loaded as he was, the task was an all but impossible one. But, added to this, the woman awakened and began talking disjointedly, sometimes crying out in fear. It was almost impossible to quiet her. She clung to him, moaning. For a whole hour he tried to assuage her terrors, until at last she dropped asleep again from weakness and weariness.

Once more Lee took up his task. Now the campfire came into view. The four men were still visible about it, shouting and quarreling; they were drunk, but not drunk enough to render escape without a fight possible.

Creeping almost inch by inch to the extension of raspberry brambles, Lee followed it to the water's edge and laid the woman down. He looked at her apprehensively for a moment, but her eyes were closed in sleep and her breathing was soft and regular.

Then coolly Lee stepped out into the open spruce and made his way toward the group. He was within twenty-five yards of them before they perceived him, and then they seemed to take him for one of their party. Lee's impressions were of confused shouting and challenging. His coolness disconcerted and bewildered them; he was almost upon them before Pierre recognized him.

'By God, it's that damn four-flusher!' he shouted.

And on the instant Lee was into the thick of them. A tall ruffian grasped a rifle and rushed at him. Lee fired. The man, shot through the hand, dropped the rifle, and, uttering a howl of pain, took to his heels in the undergrowth.

A second man was aiming at him. Lee brought the butt of his pistol down upon his head, and the man, collapsing in a mumbling heap, lay face upward upon the ground. Shorty was pulling desperately at a gun. Lee swung at him, missed his skull, but knocked him sidewise with a blow that laid his cheek open to the bone. Shorty dropped and lay still.

Pierre, who had made no movement of aggression, was staring at Lee stupidly.

'Hands up, damn you!' Lee shouted.

Pierre's arms went up to their full height. Lee frisked him, took his gun, took Shorty's and the third man's, and tossed them into the undergrowth as far as he could fling them. He stooped and picked up the rifle that the first man had dropped. And within a few seconds of the opening melee, Lee found himself, by virtue of the surprise, master of the situation.

But there was no time to be lost, for the tall ruffian who had fled was howling somewhere along the shore, and all depended upon the nearness of the motorboat. Lee, covering Pierre, backed quietly to the place where he had laid the woman. He picked her up and ran toward the boat with her. Instantly Pierre's figure was blotted out in the darkness.

Lee had set down the rifle when he picked up the woman; he placed her in the bottom of the boat, ran back and found it and threw it inside, together with the pack from his shoulders. He raised the heavy anchor. He threw all his weight against the boat, which receded in a trail of viscous mud until it was afloat. Lee leaped in, seized the oars and fired another shot in warning. All the while, the wounded man was howling along the shore.

Lee pushed desperately with the oars till he was in deeper water. He pulled furiously for mid-channel. As he did so, there came a sound that for one instant almost unnerved him, what with the psychological effect of that all-day listening to it — the chugging of the engine. Then, as he reached open water, he saw by the light of the pallid moon that issued for a moment through the storm-clouds, the black speck of the motorboat trailing the second York boat dimly.

But suddenly the rattling of the engine died in a splutter. The motorboat was about a hundred yards distant. The next instant, the bang of a rifle confirmed Lee's hopes. The engine had either run out of gasoline or had developed a fault.

Instantly Lee was pulling as he had never pulled before. Again the rifle sounded. Twice more. Now the motorboat was almost invisible in the darkness.

Then, simultaneously with another discharge, something struck Lee a violent blow in the side that knocked him on his back.

He was up in a moment, and pulling with all his might, though he knew he was wounded. But at all costs he must reach that nearing, welcome shore. He felt the wet blood trickling down him. His breath was coming in short gasps.

He bent to the oars with all his resolution set upon the completion of that journey. At last the shore seemed to reach out to him, the forests parted, the distant shouts died away. He ran the boat aground.

Lee's brain seemed preternaturally acute. In that moment he did not forget the pack, but, snatching it from the boat, leaped ashore, and running some fifty yards, placed it carefully in the brush at the base of a tall pine. He ran back, picked up the woman, and, carrying her in his arms, began to make his way into the thick of the forest.

And all the while he ran, he was weighing everything. The Free Traders would not know that he was wounded; they would certainly abandon the pursuit as hopeless. He must carry the woman a mile into the forest, where the light of their fire would not betray them, returning for the pack in the morning. He suffered no pain, and seemed momentarily endowed with some extraordinary vitality, but there was a numbness in his side which seemed to be spreading upward.

He had no idea how serious the wound was; everything that was himself was set upon the completion of the last phase of his task, so that if he died, the woman should at least come back to consciousness in the forest and not in Rathway's hands.

He struggled on, felt himself weakening; felt himself choking, and set down the woman in order to draw breath.

But as he raised her again, he felt a sudden stab of agonizing pain, and something grated beneath his heart. He realized then that the rifle bullet had split one of his ribs, probably glancing off again, and that the bone had given way under the strain of the woman's weight.

In a way this reassured him, for a glancing wound of that kind was not likely to be a serious one. On the other hand, the agony was growing unendurable. Every step was now torture. Three or four times, when it seemed impossible to proceed, Lee was forced to set the woman down and, leaning against a tree, to gasp for breath.

An eternity seemed to be passing. All his left side was now a flaming hell of pain which radiated from the wound throughout his body, and this was becoming an automaton, driven by the will. He was no longer conscious of muscular control over it. A hundred times he felt that the next step must be his last. And yet some monitor in the back of his consciousness kept insisting that he must complete the mile he had set himself, and would not let him drop in his tracks.

As he staggered on, he was surprised to hear himself talking aloud, and he listened with mild interest, as if he were overhearing the remarks of a third person.

He heard himself solemnly addressing Estelle, thanking her for having relieved him of the last vestige of the love that he had once felt toward her. He had thought he loved her once, and that love, although unworthily bestowed, had not been wholly folly. Estelle had had many good qualities of heart; she was reckless and passionate, but there was nothing petty or mean about her. She was the daughter of a well-to-do lumberman, and she had been well educated; but there was some taint in her blood that drove her upon wild and erratic courses.

For a while she had been on the stage, and had earned some reputation as a clever mimic. For a long time, Lee had known nothing of the stories that were being circulated by all the gossips of the town, nor that her name was associated with that of a man named Kean, whom he had never met. Kean was one of a gang selling liquor to the Indians, and he had a wife in Chicago.

Lee learned, about a month before the date set for their marriage, that he was the commiseration and the laughing stock of the little community. When, burning with anger, he went to confront Estelle, it was to find that she had been warned of his discovery, and had fled from the place — to Kean, the gossips said.

Lee never made any inquiries. As soon as possible he secured a transfer to another post; then he was sent to France, and his life had no room for feminine interests.

About ten months previously, however, while in the trenches, he had had a letter from Mrs. Kean enclosing a copy of a marriage certificate. She was thinking of a divorce, and wanted to know whether he could give her any information about the couple.

Lee knew nothing of either. But the letter had shaken him a good deal, as had the meeting with Estelle that day as well. What an end for her!

It was a queer personality that talked, the fragments of the man who he had once been, and Lee discovered that this lost portion of his personality was recalling to mind all sorts of queer things, quite trivial and unimportant episodes of that unhappy entanglement.

And so one part of him held colloquy with the shade of the woman who was now nothing to him, while the other held the unconscious woman, and drove the lagging body onward.

And to his horror, in that dim light the woman he clasped seemed to take on the aspect of Estelle, and he found it was to her that he was talking.

But then he heard her moan slightly, and pulled himself together. This was not Estelle, it was his comrade of the range whom he was carrying. The phantom disappeared into the past, and once more Lee was aware of that odd sense of tender companionship. He rested her head more gently against his shoulder.

At last, when he was satisfied that he had gone the mile he had set himself, he laid the woman down on the ground, and, breaking off some spruce branches, he made a bed for her and wrapped her in his mackinaw again.

And with that, it was all he could do to hold himself together while he examined his own wound as best he could. He saw that it was a mere flesh wound. The bone had taken the force of the bullet, which had glanced off, and one broken end was working into the flesh.

He tore some strips from his shirt, and having brought the ends into position, bound them tightly. And then he dropped to the ground at the woman's feet and lapsed immediately into a delirious slumber.

7

The Woman Awakens

All that night, it was the will that sustained the worn-out body in that fight up through the darkness, and the knowledge that he must retain intact the thread of consciousness if he was to save the woman from the alternative between death in the forest and recapture. At earliest dawn, he must retrieve the pack in case Rathway's men should decide to beat about the shore and so, perhaps, might find it. Beyond that point, he would not let his anticipations carry him.

It was some time before the dawn when Lee heard the woman cry out suddenly, a moan of pain and surprise as the body, heavy with its coma, struggled to convey the sense of distress to the dazed mind.

That cry drove the phantoms of delirium from Lee's mind, pulling him back to consciousness, and in an instant

Lee was at the woman's side, perfectly master of himself. As she stirred and murmured, he raised her, put his arms about her, and took her head upon his shoulder as tenderly as if she were a comrade wounded upon patrol.

But as he listened to her broken utterances, Lee realized that it was more than physical pain that was tormenting her.

'I cannot go on. It was too heavy a price. I must go back. If you won't kill him, save me and take me away. It is not that I didn't trust you, only you didn't understand . . . He looks honest, but who knows that he is? He isn't a prospector, he hasn't a pick or a pan. What should he be doing in the range? Yes, I'll go through with it. I'll go with you when he's asleep, only don't harm him. You must promise me not to harm him. Yes, he means well and wants to help me. He doesn't know who you are. You must swear that no harm shall come to him . . . '

She was living over again the events of the past. Her utterances became more broken, she moaned — suddenly she lay quiet, relapsing into the sleep of profound exhaustion.

Lee staggered to his feet and lay down once more. But this time, it was neither to sleep nor to fall back into the nether depths of delirium. He saw that a titanic conflict had been going on within the woman, and it seemed to him now that she had been going up to Rathway. Something in the conversation between Rathway and Estelle — what had it been?

He pondered over it all in a disconnected way as he lay there, still aware that another part of him was living over those days of long ago. Then at last the first light of dawn came creeping through the trees, and slowly this pain-racked, thirst-tormented being settled down into himself again.

As soon as it was half-light, he was on his feet. After looking at the woman and convincing himself that she was not likely to awake for several hours, he set off, aching in every limb, toward the shore of the lake in order to retrieve the pack.

In less than half an hour he emerged out of the forest, and, after a careful survey of the lake had convinced him that neither the Free Traders nor their boats were in evidence, he struggled down to the river and bathed in the ice-cold waters, lapping them up and feeling new life flow into his veins.

He adjusted and tightened the bandages. The broken rib was snugly held, and Lee felt that he had gone through the worst of it.

He found the pack. It contained a blanket and waterproof sheet, tea, sugar, bacon, flour, cream of tartar, salt, cornmeal, some dried apricots, matches, and nails; there were a pot, a pannikin, plate, knife, fork, and spoon, an axe and a small saw.

His wound made it impossible to carry this on his back, but with the axe in one hand Lee sliced off a number of pine branches, out of which he constructed a rough framework on which to haul the pack. An hour's work and an hour's struggle through the woods brought him back to the woman.

She was sleeping naturally, and there was a faint tinge of color in her cheeks.

After a short rest, Lee set about the task of making camp. He gathered brushwood and built a fire; he put the pot on to boil which he had brought back full of water. And, having on the return journey discovered a small clear stream nearby, he decided that that would be a safe camping place until they could proceed, and accordingly bent down some saplings and proceeded to thatch them with branches, to make a shelter for them.

He had just begun when he heard a low call behind him. The woman was awake and conscious at last. She was looking at him in wonder, but not in fear.

'Where am I? What happened?' she asked.

Lee saw at once that she had no consciousness of anything that had occurred after the catastrophe, and probably it would be some time before the memory of that came back to her. He must protect her against the shock of the realization until she was able to bear it.

'Your horse threw you,' he answered. 'You hurt your knee and cut your head. You'll have to keep still for a while, and we shall have to remain here for a few days. Are you in much pain?'

'My head aches, and my knee — yes, it does hurt a little. It isn't broken, is it?'

'It was dislocated. I had to set it.'

'Oh!' A faint color crept into her cheeks. There was a little silence. 'Are you a doctor, then?'

'No, I was just a humble orderly and stretcher-bearer on the western front,' Lee answered. 'But you see, it had to be attended to, and so I — well, I did it. After you've drunk some tea I'm going to be an orderly again and re-bandage your head.'

'But my hair — my hair! You cut my hair off!' she exclaimed, putting her hands up to her head. 'Was that necessary?'

'You were caught by your hair under your horse, and there was a danger that it might roll on you at any moment,' Lee prevaricated.

She patted her head again, felt the jagged locks about her neck, and looked at him with eyes in which a little mirth appeared.

'Thank you, Mr. Barber,' she said.

'I'm so glad you take it in that way. I was afraid you might find it difficult to forgive me.'

'I might, only — well, you see, I've been thinking of having it bobbed for some time, only I never got around to it; I don't think you made a very clean job of it, did you?'

They laughed, but she was weak, and after she had drunk the tea Lee made for her, she fell asleep until the middle of the afternoon, by which time Lee had completed the shelter over her.

'Better?' he asked when she awoke.

She nodded. 'You don't look nearly so swimmy now,' she said. 'And I'm not in much pain. But will I have to lie here on my back for days?'

'As a matter of fact, the sooner you try to walk, the better. I'm going to cut a serviceable crutch for you, and you'll be able to hobble about the camp just as soon as you feel inclined.'

'But you're not hurt, are you?' asked the woman. 'Your left arm seems stiff.'

'I hurt my side a little, but it'll be all right in a few days,' Lee answered.

She wrinkled her forehead. 'Do you know,' she said, 'I don't quite remember falling. I was riding, you say? Were we both riding? Then where are our horses?'

'They were badly hurt,' said Lee. 'It became necessary to put them out of their suffering.'

The woman was trying hard to remember. 'A bad fall, then? How did it happen? A bad fall in this forest?'

'A little distance back. I carried you here. We fell down a rocky slope.'

'Oh!' She remained silent a little, evidently trying to remember. Then she smiled. 'You've been wonderfully good to me. You know I trusted you the minute I saw you, and I wasn't the least bit frightened, waking up and finding myself alone here in the forest with you.'

'I hope you'll be able to bear the waiting here,' said Lee. 'We'll go on just as soon as it's possible.'

'But I'm not really in any hurry,' the woman answered. It was odd how reconciled she seemed to be now, and how the future had ceased to trouble her. 'It's so glorious to be in the woods again, and at this time of the year above everything. It's such a long time since I was in the woods before. I've been living in a big city, you know — nothing but blocks of houses and asphalt and stone. I felt like a prisoner there.'

And Lee wondered again at her acquiescence in this new turn of fate. 'Now — may I wash that cut in your head and tie it for you?'

'Yes, doctor.' She smiled at him.

He boiled the bandage, washed the cut in the boiled water, and retied the strip of cotton about it. The woman was still too weak to talk very much. But it was the most wonderful thing that had ever happened to him, sitting there with her in that intimate companionship, forgetting that she had been at odds with him, putting aside all the memories of conflict; forgetting, too, that she was a woman, seeing in her only a comrade.

After a while, Lee made some cakes in the ashes of the fire and cooked some bacon. The woman was able to eat a little, and he felt his appetite returning. Undoubtedly he had gone through the worst of it. Again they sat in silence, till the woman said: 'Do you know, I've forgotten your name!'

He had not told her, but he said, 'Lee Anderson.'

Anderson was a common enough name in the district, and would convey nothing to her. And as she seemed still to be fretting or puzzling, Lee laid his hand on hers and said: 'You mustn't worry. We shall go on just as soon as it's possible to.'

'That's just what I've been wondering about,' she answered. 'It's very silly of me, but — where is it that we're going?'

And, as Lee looked at her in astonishment, she went on:

'It's curious, you know, Mr. Anderson, but I don't seem exactly to remember where we met, either, or why I left that place — where was it? That big city whose name's slipped my memory for the moment. Nor why we came to the woods — came *back* to the woods, you know,' she corrected. 'And then, who am I? I had my name on the tip of my tongue a moment ago, and I'll know soon, I suppose, but it's — just now it all seems to be confused, somehow.'

And then Lee realized that her memory of the past was completely obliterated.

8

While Memory Slept

No, the woman had not completely forgotten, for it was not exactly a blank to her. She had a vague recollection of a number of things, but everything appeared to be shadowy and confused, and when she tried to piece it together, the fragments slipped out of her grasp.

It was in names and places that the lapse chiefly occurred. Including her own identity, and it was this fact that gave Lee cause for meditation.

She had lived in the forests in childhood — she seemed to recall a visit to them of recent years; at any rate, she had all the woodcraft of one to whom the forest was home. She had been educated in a convent, she thought, and had been living for several years in a large city, studying. She thought she had been studying to be a medical missionary among the Indians.

Thus she was not cut off from that association of habits, tastes, and experiences that goes to make the personality; she did not feel that she had lost very much, and it was always as if she were upon the point of remembering everything. Out of this vague, blurred dream, she had awakened to find herself in the woods with Lee, without the knowledge of how or why she had come there.

It might have been the concussion from the fall, but Lee, after pondering over the case, decided that it was much more like a case of shell-shock, and that the injury to her head had been only a contributing cause.

He made her a crutch next morning, and by the afternoon, she felt well enough to hobble a few steps about the camp. The accident which had temporarily ungeared her memory seemed to have wrought a strange change in her nature. She was no longer wildly anxious to push on to her destination; she accepted Lee as a fact in her life, and showed how completely she trusted him, despite the intimacy in which they were both living.

He was sure that her memory would suddenly come back to her completely. And, memory did come back in dreams, as with shell-shocked patients, but only to vanish with the waking. At night Lee, lying near her beneath another rough shelter of boughs that he had made for himself, would hear her tossing and moaning, and occasionally uttering fragments of unintelligible sentences.

Day merged into day. Lee's rib was healing well, and the woman was beginning to set her foot to the ground. At first she was dependent upon him in nearly everything. He helped her to take her first steps without the crutch, leaning upon his shoulder. They were always together.

It was so wonderful a companionship. It was that comradeship of which Lee had always dreamed. And it was the more wonderful, perhaps, because the woman's severance from the past gave it a sort of unreality, as if it were a little piece of paradise which they had snatched for themselves out of the sum total of human happiness.

Soon she began to assume charge of the camp and the cooking. And Lee, lying at her feet, listening while she talked, or lying awake at night beneath his shelter, in the dread of hearing her moan, came at last to realize that his feeling for her was becoming something more than the mere enjoyment of her companionship.

He loved her, he sometimes admitted to himself; and when a word or glance of his would send the blood mantling into her cheek, he dared to think that his love was returned. And now he cared no longer whether her memory of the past ever came back to her. Almost better to let her live in ignorance of all that had distressed her.

He began to dread the inevitable day when remembrance would come to blot out their paradise. Only a little incident would be needed, some little shock that would knit the raveled ends of memory, and then —

Then what would lie before them?

Another thing to be apprehended was

the day, so near now, when they must leave their woodland paradise. Autumn had returned wonderfully, but there was a sharper tang in the air each morning, everything was dead and ice formed every night upon the pool beneath their little spring.

And it seemed now as if Lee's search for Pelly would have to be protracted through the winter months. If his inquiries at the mission proved fruitless, it would mean returning to Little Falls for a sleigh and dogs.

Then there was the matter of the Free Traders. Lee would find his hands full soon enough.

'Do you know, Lee,' said the woman one day, 'I often feel as if I were on the very verge of remembering. And when I wake in the morning, just for an instant I feel a different person, as if I've remembered. And I'm afraid of remembering. It is as if remembrance would bring back something terrible with it. Who am I?'

'You're just you,' said Lee, smiling. 'That's enough for me.'

'Where did we meet?'

'In the range.'

'I was alone? And then I had an accident and was thrown from my horse? And you, too? It's so strange. I know that I lived in a large city not long ago, and that I was glad to get back to the woods, but where was I riding? That's the big problem that we have to solve, isn't it?' She looked at him earnestly. 'Lee,' she said solemnly, 'sometimes I hope I never shall remember.'

She made no plans, leaving everything to Lee, and nothing was decided. By the middle of the second week, she could walk fairly well, her strength had come back, and the little period of Elysium was drawing to its end. It was inevitable that the problem should be faced.

For the first time, she had accompanied Lee as far as the lake shore. There had been no signs of the Free Traders, and Lee was convinced that they had long since abandoned all hope of finding them. It was a wonderful evening. There was a haze of Indian summer in the November air, there was still a touch of fire in the leaves of birch and maple; the west was radiant with the sunset clouds.

And, standing there beside her, Lee knew at last — knew for sure that this love was eternal, and the former love only the pale shadow that it had cast before it. He turned toward her and read the same knowledge in her eyes.

'Dear — ' he said.

He took her in his arms, and she lay there, confident, happy in the knowledge that she was his. She put her arms about his neck and their lips met. And they looked at each other in all the thrill and glory and surprise of it. It was all so simple, and true.

'You, without a name, who have come to me out of nowhere, because I wanted you! How long have you known?'

'I've known almost since the beginning that if you cared as much as I do, Lee, you must love me more than I thought it possible.'

He looked at her incredulously, and between them the pale wraith of Estelle floated for just a moment. He had trusted her. He had vowed never to trust again in any woman. Then it was dissipated in the sunshine of their love. 'Do you care enough to trust yourself to me and take the chance of what the future may bring to us?'

'I love you enough to trust you altogether, Lee,' she answered.

But there was just the shadow of a little fear in her eyes. 'Oh, my dear, I am afraid of the time when — when I remember. I have been afraid of what may be lying in wait for us, waiting to overwhelm us, as if it grudged our happiness.'

'You must not let yourself grow morbid.' But Lee, too, felt the wings of that shadow of fear beat past him. 'There is nobody else?' he asked. 'We shall not find that we have been tricked like that? It would be unbearable.'

'No, no! I'm sure that I have never loved anybody else. I know that so well, Lee; for if there had been, I should have felt it by instinct, however deep down within me the memory of him lay buried. There is nobody but you. But what I'm afraid of is that something else, something terrible may come between us — '

'There's nothing else that could separate us.'

'If you were engaged?' Lee would no sooner have deliberately stolen another man's sweetheart than his wife; that was why the affair of Estelle had broken his life.

'Suppose I had become engaged to someone I didn't love, Lee?'

'You don't think — ' There was consternation in his voice. ' — that you — you have, dearest?'

'No, I — I'm sure I haven't. But,' she persisted, 'I just felt curious to know what we would do, in case.'

'I suppose we'd have to go to him and tell him that we loved each other, and then, of course, he'd release you,' answered Lee, looking troubled. 'Still, we don't have to think of that possibility, dear, do we?'

'Of course not, Lee,' she answered.

But again he saw that she knit her brows in perplexity, and he knew that she was thinking, thinking, trying to reunite those raveled strands of memory.

'You don't live in the range, Lee, do

you?' asked the woman presently.

'No, I live at Manistree. That's a long distance away. I've just come here on business.'

'Won't you tell me what your business is?'

Lee hesitated. 'Well, it's secret in a way, though I'm not under any pledge.' His instincts were to tell her, and yet the training of eight years seemed to seal his lips against her. 'You see, I'm acting for others.'

'Why, then of course I wouldn't ask you to tell me, Lee,' she answered. 'Only I have a curious sort of feeling that your business may be bound up with me in some way; that perhaps it means you're going into danger.'

'I don't think there's much danger attached to it.'

But she caught that 'much' with alarm. 'A little danger? You know, I couldn't bear you being exposed to danger. But — what is there beyond the range? You see, I've been talking to you about the range ever since I first heard you speak of it, and yet I don't really know where we are. It's curious, too, because for the first week after my illness, I didn't seem to care. Is there a city beyond the range?'

'No, thank God. All the cities are behind us. Nothing but forest.'

'But are you going to see someone, meet someone?'

'There's a Moravian mission three or four days' journey away.'

'Oh, are you going there?' She was still unsatisfied, still looking at him in that wistful way.

'Yes. I'm going to take you there, dear, and leave you in the care of Father McGrath, who's in charge of it while I'm away. He'll take good care of you. He's a fine man, and well known for his work among the Indians. When the old priest died last winter, Father McGrath was sent for, all the way from Labrador to take his place. I think,' he added, 'that we shall be able to start in three or four days now. We want to be off before the weather changes.'

'How long will you be away?'

'Perhaps a week — or longer.' And he wondered, as he spoke whether it would be a week — or a whole winter. He held her hands and looked into her eyes. 'Have you faith enough in me to be willing to wait quietly there even if — if I should be gone for more than a week?' he asked.

'Till you return, no matter how long, Lee,' she answered simply.

'Even if you remembered? No matter what you remember?'

'Even if I should remember. But — ' The note of fear came into her voice again. ' — when the time comes that I remember, I want you with me. I'm so oppressed sometimes — when I awake in the morning, always I seem to have been traveling in my dreams all night in horrible places, among hateful people. I seem to have some terrible duty laid upon me, something that I must carry out, although it kills me. And then — I awake to you.'

'I'll take you to the mission, dear; and when I come back, I shall take you south with me, and you shall forget all your fears,' answered Lee.

Yet, happy as he was, Lee realized that it would be well for them when he had placed her in the care of Father McGrath at the mission. Only then would the load of anxiety be removed from him.

9

Joyce Comes Home

In the middle of the night a wild storm sprang up, bringing with it a driving snow. Its violence blew down their two shelters almost simultaneously, involving them in a debris of boughs and branches.

They made light of their troubles. Lee succeeded in getting some sort of protection up, and the remainder of that night they crouched beneath it, happy, in spite of the snow that piled up all about them.

When morning came, they looked out on a white world. It was freezing hard, and the spring had dwindled to a thread in a basin of ice.

Lee very quickly had a fire burning and tea ready. But it looked as if winter had come to stay. They had had a rude awakening from their paradise. It seemed essential to push on as soon as possible.

In fact, without snowshoes they were likely to find themselves seriously inconvenienced in the event of a heavy fall. Lee meant to prosecute his inquiries at the mission, and, in case nothing came of these, to go to Little Falls, load up, and then return.

'I'm sure I'm well enough to start today, Lee,' said the woman that morning as they discussed the situation. 'We could start off slowly, you see, and then if it did snow heavily, it would be much more of a strain on me later on, without snowshoes, than now, when the traveling is easy, wouldn't it? So we ought to try to get to the mission within a day or two.'

Lee agreed, and they decided to push on slowly that day by the trail beside the lake. The mission was near the head of the lake, about two days' journey away.

Most of the contents of the pack were left behind. Lee had to travel as light as possible; but fortunately, his rib was fairly set, and the tight bandage which he wore around it eliminated serious danger of its breaking again.

When they stopped for the noon meal,

they had several miles to their credit. The woman's knee had given her no trouble, and both were jubilant. That day they covered a good fifteen miles — almost a short day's journey.

When they camped, the woman said: 'Do you know, Lee, I'm almost certain that I've passed this way before. It all looks somehow familiar to me, and yet somehow as if I'd seen it in a dream. You remember that big rock we passed in the middle of the stream? Well, I had a feeling all the time that we should come to it as we rounded the bend.'

'And you have no idea whether you ever lived in this region or not?' he asked.

'No, dear. Perhaps I was at school at that very mission you spoke of. If I was, someone there will be sure to recognize me. I've got a feeling that I was studying in some big city — Montreal or Winnipeg, perhaps, to take up medical mission work here.'

Lee did not push his inquiries. On the whole he felt it would be preferable that her memory should return to her while she was at the mission.

The next morning broke cloudy, the snow was frozen hard, and banks of heavy snow clouds were piling up in the north. The woman's knee had still not troubled her, and they made even faster progress. Early in the afternoon, the prospects of a storm became so threatening that Lee proposed they should encamp on a ridge of land some half a mile in front of them.

'We can find a safe nook in there,' he suggested.

'Oh, no,' answered the woman. 'There's a large log house about half a mile beyond that, and we'll be much more comfortable there.'

As Lee looked at her, he realized that she had been speaking without realizing what she had been saying. Suddenly she realized it too.

'Now what made me say that?' she asked. 'But I'm sure somehow that there is a cabin there. I know this place quite well, only it's as if I'd seen it in a dream. Oh, Lee, what if I should remember? I don't want to — never, never! I want our new life and our love!'

He put his arm about her and tried to

comfort her, but the look of sadness lingered on her face, and every now and then, covertly watching her, Lee would see that same perplexed knitting of her brows.

They passed the ridge, the trail ran around the bend of the lake — and suddenly they saw the log building in front of them. Lee looked at the house in surprise, for it was built in the most substantial way, and contained apparently five or six rooms. The settler who had constructed it must have meant to make it his permanent home, for the ground around it had been cleared for an acre or more; but it seemed to have been uncared for over several years, for the land was overgrown with brambles and spindly birch, into the thick of which serried cohorts of young spruce trees were advancing in ranks, like the vanguard of an army.

The door was unbolted, and when they went in they were startled at the aspect of the interior. The rooms were filled with furniture, nearly all of it made by the settler, but extraordinarily well done.

There were mildewed and faded but substantial carpets on the floors. There were fungous growths on the walls; but in spite of all the evidences of decay, the interior looked the habitation of a prosperous settler.

They went from room to room. The contents of the kitchen had been scrupulously respected, in accordance with trappers' law. There were porcelain plates, cups and saucers, cooking utensils, and a large sheet-iron stove half full of charred logs.

Lee went all over the place, calling to the woman with the enthusiasm of a boy. 'It's just the place for us!' he cried. 'We'll find out who owns it and buy it from him, and spend our honeymoon here.'

In his exuberance, he failed to perceive the depression that had settled upon her.

They had only just arrived in time to escape the storm, for already the flakes were whirling down outside.

'Well, you were right,' said Lee. 'It's lucky we're going to have a roof over us tonight. Look, here's firewood piled! Now I wonder who's been living here?'

The woman did not answer him. She was staring about her with the same look of bewilderment, and Lee saw that she was trembling. He drew her into his arms.

'Dearest, you mustn't let things trouble you,' he said. 'All will come right. And what can anything matter, so long as we have each other?'

'It makes me afraid, Lee,' she answered in a low tone. 'Oh, Lee, I — I seem to be nearer to remembering than ever before. There ought to be — there used to be a table here, and — a woman sat here sewing, a woman with fair hair, and her face bent over her work, and looking up sometimes to smile at a man — a tall man, several years older than herself, with iron-gray hair, who never smiled, but was always kind to her. And then she'd look down to smile at a child playing beside her. Was I that child, Lee?'

'If you were, if this was your home, dearest, you should be happy here.'

'I don't know, Lee. I wish now that we'd camped on the ridge. I wish I'd never come here. I've the feeling that — that it means the end.' She began to cry softly. 'It's not — not just the fear of remembering this place, but it's what is associated with it — something terrible . . . '

She ceased and looked out at the first falling snow. It was still only the middle of the afternoon, but the wind was rising, whistling about the cabin, and everything was a desolate gray. Inside the log house, it was half dark.

Suddenly the woman uttered a cry and clutched at Lee's arm. 'Lee! Did you see that? That shadow?'

Her worry communicated itself to Lee, for he had had the confused impression that a shadow had glided across the room beyond, through the open door. Instantly he darted after it, but there was nothing to be seen. He came back.

'It wasn't anything. We're getting nervous.'

'I'm sure there was — was something, Lee.' She clung to him.

'Stay here, and I'll search the place.'

'No, don't leave me! Let me go with you!'

They went together, looking into all the

rooms and about the house, but there was no sign of anyone. Lee went to the back door to look for footprints, but if any had been made, they would have been obliterated in a moment by the wind that was driving the dry snow about the doorsill in little whirling clouds.

'It was our imagination,' said Lee.

She assented, and, going into the kitchen, began to make the preparations for their meal, while Lee took the kettle down to the stream and filled it with water. But when he returned, she had ceased to work and was sitting on a chair, her head bent down, her hands clasped on her knees, staring desolately in front of her.

Lee stood beside her. 'Dearest, if I could do anything to help you — '

'You can't help me. I — I don't know what to do.'

Her voice was strained, hard; almost unrecognizable. Lee knelt at her feet, conscious of a sense of utter helplessness. He took her hands in his, and found that they were as cold as ice. Her body was strained into unnatural rigidity. It was almost as if she were a prisoner on some torture table, so set were all her muscles, as though she were bracing herself against some unendurable pain.

'Yes, you can help me!'

The words came quickly from her lips, and, raising her head, she gave him a strange, penetrating look. 'You — you haven't been frank with me, Lee. You know all that there is to know about me. But what do I know about you? You say you love me, you won my love — my love, that of the nameless woman; and you have my poor little two weeks' life story in your possession. You know everything that there is of me — oh, you know it so intimately. Can you not see how it humiliates me, to think that I have no personality of my own at all, nothing to myself, no life, hardly a thought, even, that's not yours?'

'Dearest — '

But she went on implacably: 'What do I know of you? Who are you? Lee Anderson? That's only a name. You have your life, your past. How many women has it contained, women you perhaps think of regretfully, sometimes even with tenderness — ?'

'I'd have told you that when the time came. I loved one woman. I thought I did. She was — well, I gave her my love foolishly, that's all. And it wasn't love. There is only you, has only been you.'

'How do I know you are telling me the truth, Lee Anderson?'

'You don't mean that, dear. It's just the loneliness and dread and the fear of remembering the past that makes you doubt everything. Look into my eyes and see if you can doubt them.'

The hardness of her laugh surprised him. 'I don't trust *men*, Lee Anderson.'

Lee felt stupefied. But deeper than the hurt was his pity for her, a soul cut off from the past, with only himself to guide her. He could understand that the desire for a personality of her own might well inspire her bitterness.

'I think the best way I can prove my love for you,' he answered, 'is just to say nothing till your mood has passed.'

'No, Lee, there's a better way than that, a much *better way*. Be frank with me. Let me share your life. Tell me why you came into the range, and how you found me.'

He began to tell her; but because it was impossible to speak of their experiences at Siston Lake, he made it appear that he had saved her — as he had said before — after the fall, and carried her into the woods. He omitted much, but he distorted nothing.

'What were you doing on the range? What are you here for?' Her voice was breathless; her eyes seemed to burn into his face. 'I — think — I — know. You must tell me the truth. You came here to find someone. You're a member of the police. Who have you come to find?'

And as Lee remained silent, she continued: 'It wasn't a man named Pelly, was it? An old friendless man, who had been betrayed, sold by someone he trusted? A man who had done no wrong to anyone, but who, a whole generation before, had killed the scoundrel who tried to ruin his wife? Hadn't he atoned for that by a lifetime of exile?'

'What do you *know* of him?' cried Lee.

'*He's my father!* This is our *home!* Yes,

I'm Joyce Pelly, his daughter, as you've always suspected. And *I* suspected *you* from the beginning. And you — you *forced* your presence upon me under the guise of protecting me from my friends — '

'That is not so!' Lee blurted.

' — and to gain your wretched ends by winning a woman's confidence and then *betraying her*. And you dared — yes, you dared — '

'I never dreamed who you were. Won't you believe my word of honor that I am incapable — ?'

But she went on, still implacable: 'You dared to pretend you loved me, you traitor, in order to discover my father's hiding place when I — I was coming up to him — but why — *why?* I can't remember it all. I only know that I remember I'm his daughter. And I tell you *I hate you with a hate ten times as great as the love I thought I felt for you!*'

Lee stood up before her. 'I only ask you to believe me,' he began, 'when I say that I didn't *know, guess, dream* who you were. How should I have known he had a daughter — this man I'd never seen? I knew nothing — '

But suddenly her icy coldness seemed to dissolve in helpless misery. 'Oh, leave me! Leave me for a little while, or I shall go mad!' she cried.

And she put her hands over her face and began weeping wildly.

10

The Tunnel under the Rock

Lee stumbled out of the cabin, dazed, stupefied by Joyce's revelation.

The man he sought stood, an invincible barrier, between himself and the woman he loved. Never, if he had any power to read the human heart, could Joyce Pelly look on him again with anything but hate and horror.

Beneath her gentle nature there lay, he knew, a soul of steel, calm and resolved. He could now look upon her only as a relentless enemy as long as her father lived. His little spell of happiness was ended forever.

Then to the man there came temptation fiercer than any he had known as he perceived the one way out, the only way.

It was only necessary to find Pelly, to warn him out of the district forever, to return to Manistee, making a report that

Pelly was dead, in order to win Joyce, taking her away with him, earning her gratitude, her love.

But would she love him then? Could their happiness be based on that dishonor?

Perhaps he could win her. And then? Resign from the police, of course, and bear the burden of the shame for the rest of his days, reading it in Joyce's eyes, their children reading it in their parents' eyes.

No, even that was not possible. There was no escape for him. For stronger even than conscience was the thought of the force he was so proud to serve. Those dauntless guardians of the law had endured the icy blasts of the treeless tundra; they had looked unflinchingly into the face of death, death by violence, by cold, by hunger, and on the battlefield. It was all part of the game whether one faced a moral enemy or a physical one. Even in thought there could be no tempering with dishonor.

And it was only for a moment that Lee weighed these possibilities as he strode through the storm. He would take Joyce to the Moravian mission as he had planned, there hand her over to the priest, and — leave her to go to his task, the apprehension of her father.

The storm was growing fiercer. Lee, awakening to the realization of externals as the icy flakes whipped his face, discovered that he had left the clearing far behind him; he could no longer discern the cabin in the distance through the whirling snow. He had been traveling across the ridges of the broken ground, apparently making unconsciously for the shelter of the friendly forest behind it, with the instinct of a wounded beast to take cover.

Well, he must go back, and they two must face that night together, and the next day. There was no help for it.

As he strode on, suddenly instinct pulled him up sharply. He had been trampling through a mass of withered undergrowth and bramble; and now, directly in front of him, he perceived a great gorge, so concealed in this growth that he had all but stepped over the edge.

He advanced cautiously and peered

down into it. It was an extraordinary formation. He had seen such before, in that and other regions, where the limestone, pushed up through molten granite by volcanic action at some prehistoric time, and then abraded by rain or torrent, left strange hollows and gullies. But he had never seen one on such a scale as this.

He was looking into a natural fissure in the ground; a long, irregular, winding chasm extending indefinitely into the distance, but so narrow as to be merely a lip or crack in the rugged surface of the ground. It had not been worn by rains or water; it was too deep for that. Probably the limestone, thrust up originally from the earth's inner core, had been sucked down again in some final convulsion while the granite was still half molten, leaving the granite shell about the chasm. And in spite of its depth, the chasm was so narrow that it almost looked as if a man could have leaped across it.

This was undoubtedly incorrect, the distance between cliff and cliff being only apparently reduced by the dense underbrush that fringed the orifice; but the distance between the walls, which inclined inward toward the summit, was less than half that of the base. It was just such a chasm as a man might step into in a storm, to certain death. On the floor of this gorge, Lee could see a few scrub birches standing primly erect, seeming to be hardly larger than tree seedlings in a horticultural nursery.

The fissure extended diagonally of the cabin. Lee began to retrace his steps, following it along its edge, until he came to a place where it terminated suddenly in a pile of great rocks of granite outcrop. Two of these rocks stood up, one on each side of the end of the chasm, like monoliths, although it was clear that they had not been fashioned by human hands. Between them was a third, like a monolith that had been flung down. Resting on this was an enormous rock, and Lee, who had been walking into the face of the wind, stopped and leaned against this stone for a few moments, in order to catch his breath.

To his astonishment, the massive boulder seemed about to topple backward under his weight. He felt himself slipping. He turned around, clutched at the stone, and saw it heaving under his gaze like a ship at sea.

And then he realized what had happened. The stone was not collapsing, but the pressure of his body had set it in motion. It came slowly to a standstill. Lee pressed his hand against the boulder, and immediately it was in movement again.

It was a rocking stone, and probably one of the largest in the world. The least touch started it, so delicately was it poised, but a team of horses could not have shifted it from its position.

As the huge overhanging side tilted at Lee's touch, he saw a narrow opening underneath it. His first thought was that it was that of some burrowing animal. Then he perceived that the sharp edges of the hole had undoubtedly been made by a spade. Human hands had made it. Lee stared at it until the stone, returning, hid the opening from view.

He swung the boulder again, and as it

tilted, revealing the hole once more, he flattened himself, face downward, upon the ground underneath. The stone, in its return, just grazed his shoulders.

Lee came to the conclusion that the hole extended downward beneath the base of the great stone, and, lying flat on his face, he pushed it up with his shoulders. The light that came in as it rocked backward showed him a foothold in the granite beneath the strip of mold that covered it — a rock ledge, with gaping blackness below.

Then the stone came back into position again, and nothing was visible.

Clinging in the darkness to the edges of the hole, Lee extended a foot downward. The toe of his boot struck ledge of rock. Crawling down, Lee lowered himself until he felt a second foothold beneath. Below that was a third. He found himself descending a ladder of rock.

And very carefully he began working his way downward. The granite wall was polished as smooth as glass, each foothold was precariously slippery, and he clung like a bat with hands and knees as he descended. But in a few minutes a dim light began to filter upward from below. Lee's head scraped against rock. The light grew stronger. Flakes of snow whirled in.

Then he emerged into daylight, to find himself clinging to the interior lining of the great chasm, like a fly on a wall, three-fourths of the way down. The snow was whirling about him, but the wind had ceased, cut off by the precipitous walls of the chasm.

Then Lee understood. He had found an entrance, probably the only one, into the gorge; but someone had preceded him, patiently assisting nature in the creation and enlargement of the steps of that rocky ladder, which had been eroded, during the course of millennia, by the action of a now dried-up waterfall. Only water could have hollowed out that course by the play of the leaping torrent on the projections of the granite.

Looking down from where he clung, Lee saw that a thin stream trickled over a sandy bed in the middle of the gorge below, issuing from one end, where it burst out of the granite, carrying with it the debris of the alluvial land above — mud, gravel, and sand.

And suddenly the idea occurred to him that in all probability he had stumbled upon old Pelly's gold mine. In which event, what more natural than that Pelly was hiding in that inaccessible spot, where he would he absolutely secure against discovery — unless he had incautiously permitted someone to share his secret?

And perhaps Joyce knew, and had come up in order to be with him and to procure food supplies for him. Lee gnashed his teeth at the thought of it. Fortune had played into his hands.

Lee saw that from the point where he was clinging, there appeared to be a fairly easy descent to the bottom. It was only the upper parts of the cliffs in the gorge that were unscalable. But he could go no further now. Anxiety for Joyce was rising in him. He was half afraid she might do something rash.

In some way, Rathway seemed to be associated with Pelly; perhaps he was protecting him. Suppose, then, that Joyce had gone back to the Free Traders' headquarters on Siston Lake? Or fled into the storm in her frenzy?

Suppose they had been followed? Lee remembered his fancy that he had seen an Indian watching them. The Free Traders would surely have been watching the trail at either end of the lake, knowing that sooner or later they must emerge out of the forests. Then he remembered the shadow in the log house; and this specter in which he had disbelieved, now began to assume in his mind a formidable aspect.

Suddenly, as Lee clung there, he heard a rumbling sound above his head, and a moment later something hurtled past it and smashed upon the ground of the chasm. Looking down, Lee saw the fragments of an enormous boulder lying on the ground immediately beneath him.

He had had a narrow escape. And reluctantly he turned to re-enter the tunnel. But before he had thrust his head and shoulders in, there came another rumble. And this time it was only the little projecting ledge above his head that saved his life. The boulder struck the edge of it, shot out into the air, and, just missing him, smashed to pieces below.

Lee looked up, but the cliffs shut out the view of everything except the overhanging bushes and the sky. Whether or not human agency was responsible for the fall of the two boulders, it was certain that the tunnel's mouth did not appear to be a particularly healthy spot at that moment.

Lee forced his head and shoulders through, and groped for the rock ladder within, bruising his thighs and shins against the edges of the opening. Extending his hands, he felt the smooth surface of the water-worn interior wall. He grasped the ladder, clung to it, pulled himself up, and found his footing.

And suddenly, Lee had the unmistakable instinct that he was not alone. There was another living thing within the tunnel! Though it was absolutely dark except for the faintest reflection from the interior of the gorge, which filtered up from below, and though Lee could not hear the faintest sound, he felt its presence; by some inner sense that was not hearing, he felt the rhythmical pulsations of its life.

Lee felt the fog of human hatred flung out toward him. Instinctively he knew the imminence of an encounter under conditions more nerve-racking than any he had ever experienced. He knew for sure now that the fall of the two boulders had been no accident. He had been watched, he had been seen to enter, and that watcher meant to fight him to the death. And of course it was Pelly!

He did not relish the prospect of a struggle with the crazed old man, one which could hardly end in any other way than by the death of one of them. It would be a sharp, relentless struggle, in which Lee's disadvantage lay in the fact that he could not be the first to fire.

Lee called: 'Is that you, Pelly? I want to talk to you.'

No answer came. He strained his eyes upward through the darkness. Colors and wheels of light flashed across his vision and went out.

'Pelly, listen to me!' Lee tried again.

'You know what I've come for. You've got no chance. Surrender, and you'll get fair treatment.'

Still no answer; and yet Lee could feel that other human personality close to him. He waited, baffled. There was no way to move, save vertically; and there was no possible retreat for him. The ice-smooth granite walls were all about him. The tunnel was a straight, narrow shaft up and down, from the rocking stone above to that deadly drop below.

It was impossible to rush the other, impossible to do *anything* except to clamber stiffly up those slippery rungs of rock, expecting every instant to hear the roar of Pelly's pistol and to receive the bullet in his breast. It was absurdity. And once again Lee tried:

'Pelly, you'd better give up. I can shoot you from here. Surrender, and — '

He did not end that sentence. For, as he clung there, in a moment the thing above him had materialized into life, action, fury. A bellow burst from its throat, and the sound, compressed within the shaft, and deflected from wall to wall, sounded like the roar of some prehistoric monster.

A heavy body rammed him with a force that all but dislodged him. For an instant Lee struggled wildly to retain his balance — and then there came a blow over the heart that knocked the wind out of him.

Lee's hand encountered an enormous hand at his chest. Within that hand he felt the hilt of a knife. Reaching back, Lee's fingers closed upon the last inch or two of a wide blade. The steel appeared to be buried almost to the extremity within his body.

There was no sense of a stab, but for an instant Lee felt a deadly faintness overcome him, and again he reeled and clutched for a foothold. Then he had torn the hand away, plucked out the knife, and hurled it down through the darkness of the tunnel into the gorge below.

The next instant, he was fighting the most desperate battle of his life to win through the tunnel before he bled into unconsciousness. He caught at two sinewy arms that clutched his body in the endeavor to fling him down; and, holding on by their knees and feet, the two wrestled in complete silence. Lee was no match; he could only cling on like grim death, feeling his lungs constrict under that pressure, and expecting every moment to feel his injured rib crack in his side.

His left hand encountered a groove in the rocky rung above him, and, gripping it, determined that nothing should tear his hold away, with his right fist he began hammering his assailant's face and body incessantly. His blows rebounded from the great chest as if it were made of rubber, and each blow sent the breath issuing hoarsely from the lungs with raucous wheezing that filled the tunnel.

If the other could have got Lee's left hand, he might have torn him from his hold; but his assailant put all his strength into the endeavor to force breath from his body and twist him backward, while Lee, clinging on desperately, continued to batter the face and body.

Although it was impossible to draw back his arm far enough to deliver a blow with full force, Lee's lower position gave him the advantage of equipoise over his strange assailant, and enabled him to administer fearful punishment.

For a minute or two it was problematic whether Lee could withstand the strain long enough to conquer. The great shoulders swung him from side to side in the shaft like a child, and all the while Lee, believing himself seriously if not fatally wounded, fought on with the mechanical action of a piston, dashing his fists into his opponent's face until at last groans began to burst from the other.

Then, feeling the clutch relaxing, Lee let go his hold, and standing straight up on the rung, brought both fists into play. No human being could have stood up against that fearful punishment. Lee's fists were wet with blood. The grasp about him relaxed. He redoubled the fury of his blows — and suddenly found that he was hammering at the bare face of the rock.

His assailant was gone. Faintly Lee heard the scraping of his feet on the upper ledges of the rock ladder.

Then, feeling cautiously above him,

Lee continued his ascent, until at length there came a tiny glimmer of light from above, changing into a sudden glare as of high noon.

The tunnel was empty.

The glare decreased to a glimmer. Lee understood what it meant. His assailant had tilted back the rocking stone and fled.

In another moment or two, Lee was beneath the stone. He flattened himself upon the ground and drew his automatic. He fired one shot, and before the echoes had died away, had pushed the stone back and emerged, pistol in hand.

The glare had been only in contrast to the dark of the tunnel. Outside it was melancholy twilight. Lee emerged into a solitary, snowbound world. There was no sign of his antagonist, who had evidently had enough for the present.

Lee looked down at the fragments of shirt that remained to him, expecting to find himself soaked in blood. He was astonished to see only a thin thread on his chest. He tore the rag open.

There was only a scratch on the skin from the knife-point, but there was a spreading bruise — under the thick coils of Joyce's hair, in which the knife blade had become entangled.

The blow, struck immediately over the heart, would have killed him instantly but for that. Lee raised the tresses reverently to his lips. And with a deep feeling of tenderness, he began to make his way through the twilight toward the log house.

He was torn between apprehension for her and speculation as to his assailant. His first thought had been that the man was Pelly. But now he began to doubt this. An old man might have had his assailant's strength, but he would not have had the endurance. Stronger still was the conviction that that massive form which had attacked him in the shaft could never have been the father of Joyce. Yet who but Pelly knew the secret of the mine?

The problem was at present insoluble, but its consideration brought with it the fear that Joyce might have been attacked as well. Lee quickened his footsteps through the storm, which was now subsiding, though the snow still fell steadily. He blamed himself bitterly for having left her. Surely the strength of that love and tenderness he felt toward her would reach her, and she would respond!

And he planned what he would say to her. He would advise her that it was improbable that her father would receive anything but a nominal sentence; that he might even go free; that in the absence of witnesses, a conviction might prove impossible. His best course would be to surrender. Lee began to grow more hopeful.

The log house came into sight, standing bare and bleak in the snowy wilderness. There was no light within.

Lee's alarm increased. He hurried to the door. He called, but no answer came. He struck a match. By the tiny light, he saw that the kitchen and the adjacent room were empty. He began going from room to room, striking matches and calling to Joyce, knowing all the while the futility of it. She was not in the house.

She had fled into the snow, and, desperately weary as he was after his encounter, Lee had no alternative but to take up the quest. She could not have gone far, but she must have been in a state of desperation to have gone out into that storm. Which way? The falling snow had surely long since obliterated her footprints.

He made his way down toward the trail beside the river. Only two ways were possible: one ran toward the mission, nine or ten miles away; the other in the opposite direction to the Free Traders' headquarters.

But suddenly Lee's hopes and spirits leaped up confidently. Stooping, he traced the tracks of a sleigh along the trail. It had been drawn by a single horse, and it was going in the direction of the mission. There was only one reasonable inference: Father McGrath must have been passing. Perhaps he had met Joyce, and he had taken her with him.

Lee took up the long walk immediately. The snow was deep, progress was difficult without snowshoes, and the frost had already crusted the surface, so that his feet sunk in cumbrously at every step. But a great load was removed from his mind;

the future now looked roseate.

At last the mission came into sight — a group of log huts clustered about a larger one on a low elevation, surrounded by the forest. Lights gleamed pleasantly inside them. A horse was neighing in some stables.

Lee strode up the ascent and hesitated as to which hut to approach; stood irresolute for a moment in the open space at the crest of the little hill. Then as he waited, the door of one of them was flung open, and a man in a mackinaw and lumberman's boots stepped out toward him. Under his arm he held a rifle. He presented it at Lee's breast.

He looked to be about fifty years of age, or a little older. He had a round smooth face as soft as a babe's, and an incipient paunch. A silver cross hung from his mackinaw. A jolly-looking priest; but the eyes within the face were steel-gray and cold. He stopped two paces distant.

'Take yersel' off, ye damned Free Trader,' he said softly, 'or I'll blow ye into Kingdom Come!'

11

'If You Find My Father'

Lee spoke quietly. 'I want to see Miss Pelly.'

'Aye, ye want to see Miss Pelly! But ye canna see her and ye wilna see her.'

'Will you give Miss Pelly my message?'

'Will ye take yersel' away?'

'No!'

McGrath flung down the rifle. 'Come on, then; come on, ye swine of a hooch peddler!' he shouted, brandishing his fists.

Lee flung up his arm just in time to protect himself against a straight right that would have knocked him senseless. The next moment Father McGrath's arms were locked around him, holding him as if in a vise.

'Will ye take yersel' away before I'm tempted to forget my calling?' the father panted.

'Father McGrath — '

'I'll have no dealing with ye and your nest of iniquity. I'm no afeard of all the Free Traders that ever come out of hell. I'll send ye back to the devil before your time, if you come meddling with my mission. I've made my compact with your master, as I'd make a compact with the evil one himself, to protect my bairns. Mebbe ye're a new hand — I don't remember your face — so I'll remind ye of it. Ye're to be free to peddle your filthy liquors where ye will — aye, an' I dinna doubt the good Lord will score it again ye too, for shamin' His good corn whisky by mixin' in your filthy wood alcohol the way ye do — ye can peddle them where ye please, but ye'll leave my lasses and weans alone, or I'll make Siston Lake too hot to hold ye.'

'Father McGrath — ' Lee tried again.

'Will ye fight, man to man, ye doomed Free Trader? Will ye fight or wrestle with me?'

'I'd be glad to, Father, but just now one of my ribs is broken. When I get better, perhaps.'

Father McGrath released him. 'Ye're speakin' the truth? Well, then, take yersel' off. Ye canna see Miss Pelly.'

A light footstep sounded beside him. Joyce stood there. Lee swung toward her. 'I came to make sure you were safe. Joyce . . . ' Lee held out his arms.

'Dinna speak to him, Miss Pelly. I understand he's helped ye — aye, there's good in the worst of us — but he'll get around ye, Miss Pelly. Go back!'

'Father, there's something I want to say to him,' Joyce answered in a low voice.

'Aye, but he's got a smooth tongue, and the stamp of iniquity hasn't come upon his face yet. Ye wouldna think he'd sold himself to his master. If ye must speak to him, I'll just standby, and if I see he's getting 'round ye, I'll send him about his business.'

With which the doughty father took up his post just out of hearing, glaring at Lee and prepared for instantaneous intervention. Joyce stepped forward.

'Lee, I — I'm sorry for what I said to you this afternoon. It was partly the shock of awakening, I think. I was unjust to you, and unjust, too, in coming here without trying to get word to you. I owe you a great deal. I accept your word that when you met me in the range you didn't know who I was; that you didn't pursue my acquaintance because I was the daughter of the man who it was your duty to apprehend. I — I bear you no ill will for having to do your duty.'

'Then, Joyce — '

'But,' she said solemnly, 'you'll see how my father's safety, perhaps his life, stands between us. We can only be enemies — at least, until — '

'That's what I wanted to speak about,' said Lee. 'As I understand it, this killing was committed years ago, a whole generation ago. It was more or less justified. If your father is brought to trial and convicted, it will almost certainly be for manslaughter. His sentence will be a nominal one. Quite probably it will be impossible to produce the witnesses required to convict at all. In which case, he'd go free. He's acted ill-advisedly. He should never have fled. His best course will be to surrender. He'll find himself a free man in a little while, instead of a hunted outlaw. Will you unite with me in persuading him to surrender?'

She shook her head. 'We always told him that — my mother and I,' she answered. 'But the thing had crazed him; he hated civilization after it happened. He was insane upon that subject. He'll never surrender.

'Let me explain to you what happened, and the treachery and faithlessness that have always pursued him. When my father fled from the law, he came here and settled with my mother. I was born here. For a long time we were very happy. My father trapped, and in those days this was one of the richest fur districts in Canada.

'But my father was an educated man, and in his heart he was always chafing against his exile. He always cherished the hope someday to take us south where I could be educated properly. Then in an evil day, he fancied he'd discovered a gold mine.

'It became a mania with him. He'd tell no one where it was, except Jacques Leboeuf, an old servant, who he trusted.

161

They used to go off by night and work it together. My father was always talking about the gold he'd collected. He wanted to develop the mine, to sell it for a fortune, but he was always afraid of being discovered, and he put it off and put it off; and neither my mother nor I ever believed in the mine.

'Then one day a man called Rathway came up. He was a small whisky peddler who had committed some crime against the Indians. He'd been beaten, pursued, and was half dead when my father saved him from their vengeance. He took him in and fed and protected him. Rathway learned of the mine, and was always searching for it, but neither my father nor Leboeuf would tell him where it was. Once he tried to spy on them, and Leboeuf had him by the throat and would have killed him if my father had not intervened in time.

'My mother died. Rathway grew fat and consequential, living here, helping my father with his traps; and though for a long time my father didn't know it, he continued debauching the Indians with his whisky. When I was a woman of seventeen, he began to take notice of me. He said he loved me. I didn't know much about love, but I knew I hated him. Then one day my father came in from the woods just in time to protect me from him, and he shot Rathway through the arm.

'He was aiming again to shoot him through the heart, for he was terrible when his anger was roused. Then Rathway, standing and facing him with his arm dripping blood, coolly told him he knew that my father had committed one murder already, and that the facts were in his possession, written down and left for safety with a friend in the south. The change in my father was dreadful. He dropped his rifle, seeming almost demented. His fears for my future, conflicting with his fears for the present and his fears of Rathway, broke his will.

'After that, Rathway stayed on and on, and they were always talking together. Rathway threatened my father, but still my father refused to show him the mine, in spite of his threats. My father wanted all of the gold for me — it was his mania.

'Once, Leboeuf came to my father and offered to kill Rathway. But my father refused, and Leboeuf, who was devoted to him, never thought of disobeying his strict command. That happened before the Free Traders were organized in Montreal, but already the hooch sellers were getting together. They'd established a number of posts, one of them at Lake Misquash, miles away, a week's journey north of here. Rathway went to Lake Misquash to confer with them. As soon as he was gone, my father seized the opportunity to send me away south to a convent to be educated.

'He wouldn't touch the hoard of gold which he claimed to possess — we'd never believed in it — but he had made money by his furs. I was to be well educated. I spent three years at the convent, and then I went to a missionary training school to study medicine, because it had always been my dream to teach the Indian and mixed-breed children in this district. And then — '

She stopped and looked at him doubtfully. Father McGrath strode toward them.

'He's gettin' round ye!' he cried. 'I can see the softenin' in your face, Miss Pelly!'

'No, no, Father!' cried Joyce sharply. 'Leave us a few minutes more!'

Father McGrath withdrew, muttering, after a doubtful glance at her.

'And then — I can't remember, Lee,' Joyce continued. 'There's a blank, a terrible blank in my mind still. The next thing I remember, I was riding north alone, to save my father, because that devil Rathway had betrayed him. But how was I to save him? That I don't know. I remember that I was half crazed with anxiety. I remember seeing you at a hotel, and those two dreadful men.

'And — they had some power over me, and I wanted you to help me, and dared not ask you. I didn't know what to do. Once, in my despair, I begged you to kill Rathway, to save my father. But how could that have saved him, when he was already betrayed?' She looked at Lee in anguish. 'Oh, I don't understand!' she cried. 'If I could remember! It was something terrible, something that I could never go through again.'

'Do you think,' asked Lee, 'that you'd pledged yourself to marry Rathway in order to save your father's life?'

'I — I couldn't have. No, never, Lee!' she trembled. Lee stepped to her.

'Joyce, nothing has changed. You're still mine.'

'Lee, it can't be. My father stands between us — will always stand — '

'Joyce, I've been thinking of something on the way here tonight. We both wish to do what's best for your father. Let's work together. Marry me!'

'Lee, it can't be — not till — '

But she swayed toward him. In a moment they would have been in each other's arms. It was a bellow from Father McGrath, whom they had forgotten, that forced them guiltily apart.

'He's got 'round ye, and I knew it would come about!' he cried. 'Get ye back to your devil's work!'

'Oh, Father,' cried Joyce, half sobbing and half laughing, 'this isn't one of

Rathway's gang. I've tried to tell you — '

'Aye, and ye told me that ye wouldna see him, and now ye'd have bussed him if I hadna stopped ye! Well, I ken the pertinacity of the devil's agents.'

'Listen to me, now!' said Lee, taking Father McGrath by the arm. And, ignoring the good priest's impulsive interruptions, he told him their story. Before he was halfway through, Father McGrath was listening in profound, perplexed astonishment.

'Father, I want Joyce to marry me,' cried Lee. 'Once she's mine, we can face the future together, whatever it may bring forward. There's no real antagonism — '

Father McGrath shook his head in perplexity. 'I canna understand it,' he said. 'I ken but little of what's been happening here. I'm a new man in the district. It isna' as if I'd known Mr. Pelly himself, you see. I canna imagine what Miss Pelly intended to do when she was coming up to see her father. Was it your intention to warn him, do you think?' he asked her. 'Or was it something more?'

Joyce could not answer him, and Lee

saw how it distressed her to try to remember. It was from that crux of the problem that the mind had withdrawn itself, refusing to remember.

'Ye were going to the Free Traders?' Father McGrath persisted.

'Oh, I don't know — I don't know!' cried Joyce in agony.

Father McGrath cleared his throat. 'It's my opinion,' he said, 'that until we discover Mr. Pelly, or learn that he's dead or away from the district, it wouldna be advisable for ye and Miss Pelly to marry unless her memory comes back to her. Mebbe I'm too conservative, but a while ago she hated ye.'

'Father, I never hated him!' cried Joyce indignantly.

'And I'm no' in favor of these quick changes,' said Father McGrath.

Joyce sided with him. 'Lee, dearest, until one of those two things happens, we must just wait,' she said. 'But if you find my father — and I'm convinced now that it would be for the best — well, then, I — I'll marry you if you want me, Lee.'

And this time there was no Father

McGrath to interfere with them, for the good priest was patting the head of an Indian baby at the door of one of the huts.

And, late though the hour was, Lee, declining the father's offer of hospitality for the night, set off for the log house again. He wanted to be alone with his singing heart in the silence.

He reached his destination sometime in the small hours, and, careless of possible attack by the mysterious wanderer, flung himself down in one of the rooms, and lay like a log until awakened by the sunlight streaming in.

Jumping up, completely rested and restored, he ran down to the river, plunged into the ice-cold waters, raced back over the frozen snow, and dressed.

Joyce was to remain at the mission until Lee knew definitely whether or not her father was in the district. Before leaving the night before, Lee had drawn the father into a talk, and had learned from him that she would not be in danger from the Free Traders. The father had been compelled, he said, much against his will, to come to an understanding with them, by which he undertook not to attempt to interfere with their operations provided his women and bairns were left alone. The board of missions was a power that the Free Traders were not anxious to tackle. Father McGrath, hating the necessity of making terms with Rathway, had felt nevertheless that he was doing the only thing possible under the circumstances, until the government made a move to wipe out the organization. He assured Lee that Rathway and his men would not dare to molest Joyce, and furthermore, that he would protect her with his life if necessary.

Lee had thought best to say nothing to Joyce about his discovery of the mine, but he meant to make a thorough search of the gorge for Pelly. Failing him, he meant to discover his mysterious assailant, in the belief that he could provide him with the clue he needed. He had no doubt that Pelly's gold mine lay in the chasm.

After having breakfasted, he made his way to the rocking stone, and slipped quietly into the tunnel. Striding a match or two, and assuring himself that it was empty, he descended, and within a minute or two had reached the lower orifice, and found himself again clinging to the interior wall of the chasm.

Here the artificial excavation of the rungs ended, but there was a fairly easy descent down the lower portion of the cliffs, which afforded plenty of hold for the hands and feet. Lee quickly scrambled down, and, swinging free of the wall, found himself standing at the bottom of the gorge, whose inclining walls shut him off completely from the sight of anyone above. Only by standing in the very center of the defile could he see the summit of the cliffs, with their dense covering of scrub.

The base of the chasm was a little wider than he had supposed, perhaps fifty paces across between wall and wall. Along the center a thin stream trickled over a sandy bed, issuing from one end of the chasm, where it burst out through the granite, carrying with it the debris of the alluvial land above — mud, gravel, and sand. This sandy deposit, carried along by the stream, had been heaped up, probably in times of overflow, against the granite walls, and within the little limestone caves that studded their lower surfaces.

Looking about him, Lee saw that some two or three hundred yards from the place where he had emerged out of the face of the cliff, the gorge made a sharp bend almost at right angle, and here the ground was strewn with a mass of fallen boulders ranging from huge rocks to small debris. Above it was a gap in the lower section of the cliff, from which it had been detached.

Lee made his way in this direction. At once he came to the conclusion that dynamite had been the cause of this collapse of part of the surface of the granite wall, which, smooth as a steel lining, could have been disrupted by no natural force such as gravity.

And then he came upon something that confirmed the obvious deduction. It was a rotting wooden cradle. Beside it lay a rusty pick. Not far away were two huge iron pans, their bottoms eaten out with rust, so that they resembled fretwork in steel. Under them were still the ashes and charred residue of the wood that had been used to thaw out the frozen earth.

All about among the fallen rocks were mounds, the residue from the pans after the extraction of the gold, now covered with tangles of dead vegetation.

There was no longer any doubt that this was Pelly's gold mine. Before making further investigations here, Lee decided to explore the remainder of the chasm. It ran on beyond the bend for a quarter of a mile, and then came to an abrupt termination. Without any gradual lessening of the depth, it simply ceased, the two cliff walls coming together in the same way as they did near the rocking stone at the other end. The chasm was, in fact, simply an elongated crater.

Returning, Lee made his way to the cave formed by the explosion. If Pelly was in the district, there was hardly any doubt but that he would be hiding in that inaccessible spot, where he would be safe against discovery. It was not unlikely that he was in the cave itself at that moment.

Lee first examined the snow about the

mouth of the cave for footprints, but he found no tracks except his own. Drawing his automatic, he advanced into the opening. The sand in the interior bore the marks of continued trampling, but there were no imprints with clear edges, and it was certain that no one had been there for a long time.

Unfortunately, Lee had brought no candle, but he advanced some distance within the cave, lighting his way with matches. However, it was a foregone conclusion that Pelly was not in there, for the sandy interior bore no fresh footprints as far as he went.

A faint, distant roaring as of a waterfall came to Lee's ears, and the air was fresh, as if the cave were connected with some opening in the mountain side. Lee resolved to explore it another day. But it was clear enough that Pelly was not in the chasm after all. Another thing that led Lee to that conclusion was the fact that no mining operations had been carried on there for a considerable time — long enough for the pans to have rusted through.

If Pelly had taken refuge within the gorge, it was incredible that he would not have resumed operations. And these seemed to have been interrupted unexpectedly, to judge from the exposure of the pans to wind and weather.

Perplexed and disappointed, Lee turned his thoughts toward the capture of the man who had attacked him in the tunnel. He could no doubt throw light on Pelly's whereabouts. Perhaps he was the assistant of whom Joyce had spoken.

Lee expected that he would be lurking in the tunnel, ready to renew his attack; but this time there should be no such fiasco as before. He made his way back on the opposite side of the gorge, where there was a thick growth of dwarfed scrub laurel which had taken root in the soil brought down by the little stream, and bordered it, extending back from it toward the cliff in a sort of miniature jungle. Something protruding out of this growth arrested Lee's attention.

It was a wooden cross carved with the name HELENE PELLY, standing up above a low cairn of boulders.

Lee stood and looked, and vaguely mournful thoughts coursed through his mind. It was a sad and lonely burying place for Joyce's mother. Its existence there was in itself a testimony to the old man's mental condition — that he should have carried his wife's body through the tunnel to that place of his dreams. And yet it was certain that no prowling thing would ever violate that grave.

Lee went on, and, a few steps further, stumbled against something else. It was the skeleton of a man, the bones protruding through the rents and tatters of the scarecrow clothes. The laurel tangles sprouted between the ribs. The bones were bleached white; the flesh had long since disappeared. One bony hand still tightly clutched the handle of a large old-fashioned revolver. The muzzle was choked with rust; there were rusted cartridges inside.

Disengaging it with difficulty from the fingers, Lee saw, on the less rusted portion of the handle which they had protected, the initials C. P. But he hardly needed that to know that his mission was at an end, and the last barrier between himself and Joyce overthrown. The problem so inscrutable an hour before had been solved. All cause for antagonism between them had come to an end.

Lee was conscious of a quiet satisfaction. It was the happiest solution, and though Joyce would grieve, she would come to see that it was the best. She would be glad, after the first shock, that her father would not have to face the ordeal which he had dreaded for so many years.

But as Lee looked down at the remains of the dead man, he became aware of a single fact. Nearly every bone on one side of the skeleton was broken — the skull, ribs, arm and leg bones, and pelvis.

Then Pelly had not died of a stroke or from a sudden attack of heart failure. He had fallen from the summit of the cliff above — perhaps he had been flung down, for the revolver which he had been clutching showed that he had either encountered or anticipated an enemy.

Filled with a mixture of emotions — happiness for their future, grief for the news that he must break to Joyce — Lee made his way toward the tunnel.

But all at once he made the singular and unexpected discovery that he did not know where the entrance was.

12

Freed by a Lock of Hair

It seemed to him that it would be a simple matter enough to ascend the cliff again, and he had not taken the precaution to take note of landmarks. Now, however, he discovered that the lower third of the granite wall was scored with hundreds of holes and fissures where the friable limestone had crumbled away, or had been washed out by the streams. The entrance to the cliff tunnel was somewhere on that side of the chasm, some little distance from the bend — but where?

Lee stepped back to the brink of the stream and looked up, trying to locate the rocking stone or monoliths for a guide, but the upper incline of the cliff hid them from view.

It was high noon. Lee set himself to the task before him. He looked about him, trying to orientate himself. It would be necessary to ascend to a point about one-fourth the distance up the cliff in order to discover the ingress, which was no wider than any of numerous cavities in the wall.

Plenty of places along the chasm afforded access, and Lee grasped a projecting rock which seemed familiar, and began to ascend, digging his hands and feet into the holes, until he found it impossible to proceed farther. Swinging to the right, he discovered a large cavity and thrust his arm in up to the shoulder.

A bitter disappointment awaited him, however, for at the end his hand encountered only a smooth surface of rock.

He tried again as he descended, thrusting his arms into all the likely crevices in the vain attempt to find the orifice.

He descended, selected another place and scrambled up the wall again, only to achieve the same negative result. And when he reached the bottom of the cliff again, and looked up at the innumerable crevices, he realized that not only did he not know at which point to begin the ascent, but he did not know how high to climb before he reached the level of the tunnel entrance.

He looked up at the huge cliff, with its inward incline and scored with its myriads of mocking mouths, and now a sort of fury took hold of him. Again and again he scrambled up and clung like a fly to the cliff's face; scrambled down, baffled, and then began once more.

It was now the middle of the afternoon, and he was no nearer a solution. He had accomplished nothing. He was becoming bewildered. It was necessary to proceed in a systematic way.

He now proceeded to mark off what he considered the possible boundaries within which the tunnel lay by stamping down two birch saplings. And again and yet again he essayed his task, always to recoil, beaten.

He was only halfway from sapling to sapling, and it was beginning to grow dark. His hands were bleeding, his nails split to the quick. But it was the eerie nature of his efforts in the loneliness of the darkening gorge that was the most nerve-racking part of all. He was like some mythical hero of the classical world, tortured by inanimate things — like Sisyphus, condemned to roll his stone up the hills of Tartarus forever, only to have it bound down again before it reached the summit.

He had been toiling by moonlight for an infinity of time and had covered all the space between the saplings. He extended his radius; and now, in his desperation, he attacked the cliff as if it were a human enemy, beating on it with his fists in senseless fury.

Dawn, clear and gray and bitter cold, crept into the gorge and found him still at his labors. The sun rose. Long rays of light streamed down into the chasm, in which Lee struggled like a madman, dust-white, disheveled, haggard, half-delirious from want of sleep and exhaustion.

He stopped and tried to collect himself. But to cease meant to yield to despair. Only by incessant labor could he keep up the pretense that he was about to find the tunnel. He felt at the end of his resources. One conclusion was being borne in upon him: he had worked his way far beyond the saplings on either side; he must have passed the tunnel during the night.

One little orifice unexplored in the obscurity, and all his work had gone for nothing. He would have to go back to the beginning and start over again. But no human being could go through the test again.

There occurred to him an alternative, but so fantastic that he only played with it as a madman plays with a straw. The tunnel might be no longer there. It might have disappeared through a rockslide.

That seemed incredible — Lee put the thought from him; its very occurrence made him realize that his mind was beginning to wander. Lapping up some water from the stream and sprinkling himself with it, he began again, at the farther sapling.

The sun rose high. It was beginning to descend. It ceased to illuminate the gorge. Lee was nearing the second sapling. He would work on till that was passed, and then — what?

Now each step of each ascent was an incredible labor. His hands were lumps of bruised flesh. He was hardly conscious what he was doing. Still, he must reach the second sapling.

He passed it. A sort of film descended over his consciousness. In the declining day, he saw himself staggering around the gorge, seeking for some other egress. Impossible! For forty feet there were footholds innumerable in the lower part of the cliffs; above them the hard granite surface bulged inward. There was no handhold for an ape. And he staggered from one end of the gorge to the other, 'round and 'round and 'round — an ape in a cage . . .

He dropped upon the ground utterly worn out, utterly hopeless. A little respite, and then he would arise, to struggle again. A short sleep . . .

Respite? He had slept, and that lynx sense of his had just awakened him in time — just in time to anticipate that shadow stealing down the gorge toward him. It leaped forward, snarling, and then leaped back as Lee struck at it.

Lee was alert on the instant. In that thing alone lay his chance of escape. And, as it vanished into the shadows, Lee went blundering after it in the darkness, finding it, losing it. He saw it in every moon-shadow among the rocks. He heard it jeering at him. Then stones began to fly. One grazed his cheek, one struck him in the chest. Now the thing was in front of him, and when he rushed, it was not there, and a shower of stones from an unexpected quarter cut his lip and chin.

Thus tortured, maddened, Lee was baited till the second dawn filtered into the gorge. There was no respite. All the while, Lee struggled against the bonds of sleep. He would rest, his eyes closing for an instant — it was upon him again, a stone would hurtle past him; another rush would follow, and again the thing was gone in the dark.

Dawn — daylight — sunlight. Crouched behind a ridge or rock above him, Lee saw the figure with the massive shoulders. Yielding to the elemental rage that was in him, he whipped out his automatic and fired two bullets. They chipped fragments of stone from beside the face, which continued to watch him unmoved. Lee pulled the trigger a third time, but there was no third shot. Then he remembered that he had had only two cartridges remaining. He was unarmed.

He sprang, and a stone struck him in the chest and hurled him backward. Like two baboons, they bombarded each other with stones; but at last, as a fortunate shot sent the other staggering, Lee managed to close with him. The face, bruised and battered from the encounter in the tunnel, looked impassively into his. Lee struck, and quickly discovered that he had not strength enough left to administer a knockout blow; while at close quarters he was decidedly at a disadvantage.

On the other hand, his opponent was equally unable to overcome him, for he could not stand up against Lee's fists at short range long enough to allow him time to get the gripping power of those shoulders into action. At last, bleeding and bruised, they broke off the fight simultaneously, and lay side by side, panting, upon the bottom of the gorge.

Lee took stock of the other. The man looked like an Indian, but there was a touch of the Caucasian in him. Lee addressed him for the first time.

'What is it that you want? Why have you attacked me?'

The answer — Lee had hardly expected that there would be an answer — was in a tone singularly soft.

'You find the way in. But you never find the way out. You fight me and I fight you. You sit down here so and I sit down here beside you so. When you fight I fight, and when you stop I stop, and so we wait until you sleep. And then *le grand mort* come.'

This devilish conception made Lee's blood run cold. For even now, his eyelids were drooping — drooping, and the other watched with cunning eyes. He tried to find strength to leap, rend him with teeth and nails if his bruised fists and weakened arms failed him. But the other, reading what passed in his mind, crouched, ready for him.

Lee shot an arrow at a venture. 'Leboeuf?' he said softly.

The other started. 'Eh, you have learn my name? That makes no difference.'

'Why do you wish to kill me? Is it that you think I've come here to seize the mine?'

'Listen, then. I swore to my master before he died that no one shall take the gold away. Therefore, since you have found the way into the tunnel, you shall never leave it.'

'Suppose I'm a friend?'

'No, no friend. You've come for the gold. You came to seize my master, who is dead, to take his gold away. There he lies dead, and he has come to me in dreams and told me he must not be buried till Mam'zelle Joyce has got the gold. Aye, you shall never have his gold.'

'Listen, Leboeuf! Miss Joyce and I love each other — '

'No, no, you are lying! And, besides it would make no difference. Did I not hear her in the house, telling you, 'Go! Go!' No, you shall never take her gold.'

Lee desisted from sheer weariness. He strove desperately in his mind, trying to find some way by which he could convince this madman — but his eyelids closed, and suddenly with a snarl, Leboeuf was upon him, his fingers twining around his throat.

Lee shook himself free. He sprang at him, the last of his waning strength put forth. They clinched, they fought; Lee's fists beat against the bruised face, drawing fresh blood. Leboeuf released him, but springing to a distance, began hurling stones at him, cursing him. Then he sat down and waited.

Lee must stay awake till nightfall. He would find some way out of the gorge. He would cut footsteps in the granite with a stone; such wild and impossible thoughts ran through his mind. He strode to and fro beside the riverbank.

Some little distance away, Leboeuf sat watching him. Lee's hatred for that bruised, impassive face was elemental. He flung a stone. The aim was true; it cut Leboeuf's lip open. Blood began to drip, but Leboeuf never stirred.

Lee sat down. He must conserve his strength — he started up. He had slept for a moment, and Leboeuf was creeping toward him. The sun blazed over the edge of the gorge. A moment later, Leboeuf was almost at his side, yet he was not conscious of his having moved, or of having closed his eyes. He got up wearily, picked up a stone, and flung it into Leboeuf's face, gashing his cheek.

Leboeuf never moved.

Lee looked about him for a larger stone.

He was lying upon his back, and Leboeuf was kneeling on him, gripping his throat. He tried to struggle. The wiry fingers ripped the tatters of his shirt away.

The next moment, a cry broke from Leboeuf's lips. He was fingering the coils of Joyce's hair. He knew them, perhaps by the faint odor of her that clung to them.

He fell upon his knees. 'Monsieur, it is hers! Forgive! Forgive! I am an old fool! So among my people the maidens give their hair as tokens of love! Ah, monsieur, monsieur — see, I will show you the entrance, and you shall take the gold for her. So my master spoke in a dream — but I did not know you!'

And, darting from Lee's side, he scrambled straight up the face of the cliff between the saplings. He dragged away a stone, fitting so closely into the tunnel's mouth that Lee had never guessed it had been placed there. And, with a mournful cry, Leboeuf disappeared within the tunnel.

Lee staggered to the cliff beneath it, tried to ascend, dropped back, and in a moment was fast asleep upon the bottom of the gorge.

13

And on the Day after Tomorrow

Lee slept the clock around, for when he awoke, refreshed and restored except for his bruised and blistered hands, the sun was in the same part of the sky as when he had gone to sleep.

For a few moments, the memory of that grotesque struggle seemed like something that he had read in a book. Then, bit by bit, it began to become a part of memory's records.

But it was not until, looking up, he saw the entrance to the tunnel plainly visible in the cliff overhead, that he realized the whole episode had not been a disordered dream born of his frantic, futile struggles.

And even then, Lee could not convince himself until he had gone back to Pelly's skeleton and ascertained that it was really there, and looked at the initials on the butt of the revolver, and stood beside the little grave.

Then, very painfully, for his hands were skinned and raw, Lee clambered up the cliff and made his way through the tunnel. He did not think he would ever want to visit Pelly's gold mine again. He had suspected all the while that the mine was a myth, and even now he was not convinced that there was gold in it. But joy was in his heart, joy overflowing, for all his troubles were at an end. He was going to Joyce, to make her his wife, to take her away.

His heart thumped at the anticipation of that incredible dream, and he trod the trail toward the log house like a boy. He broke his long fast with a moderate meal and started for the mission. As he went up the ascent, a mob of mixed-breed and Indian children came pouring out of the schoolhouse. There in the entrance, Joyce was standing, watching them — and him, approaching.

She looked up at him gravely as he drew near, and she knew at once from the look on his face enough to make the breaking of the news less of a shock to her. But the tears rolled down her cheeks as he told her of her father's death.

'Joyce, darling. I can't help feeling that it's the best thing in the end,' said Lee. 'At least his sufferings are over.'

'I think so, too, Lee,' she answered calmly. 'Somehow I've always known my father was no longer alive. The bond between us was very close, though I was away from him so many years.'

Lee told her about the discovery of the mine and his encounter with Leboeuf, slurring over the story of the Indian's attack on him. Then Joyce caught sight of his hands, and was all sympathy and dismay, and took him into a hut and bathed them and bandaged them.

Father McGrath had gone to visit an old Indian in the neighborhood, and the two talked a long time, and then ate a simple meal together in the presence of the children, who stared at Lee over their soup dishes out of their large black eyes.

'It's strange, the mine being so near the house,' Joyce said. 'You know, Mother and I were never quite convinced that there *was* a mine. We were never quite sure that my father hadn't a delusion on that subject, and that Leboeuf, who was devoted to him, wasn't humoring him. Old Leboeuf must have been living there for a long time. He had some grudge against Rathway, you know. He would have killed him once if my father hadn't intervened.' She reverted to her father's death, and Lee was reluctantly compelled to give her the particulars.

'He may have suffered a stroke and have fallen over the cliff,' he said. 'At any rate, his death was instantaneous. You may be sure he didn't suffer.'

It was when he spoke of his discovery of her mother's grave that Joyce showed signs of breaking down. 'She was ill such a long time,' she said. 'She was paralyzed, and there was nothing that could be done for her. When she died, my father and Leboeuf carried her body away into the forest by night. They'd never tell me where she'd been buried, and I remember I used to prowl about the house, always hoping to discover her grave. I suppose that was a part of my father's madness. In a way, he wanted her to be near him where he was working.'

It was after dinner that Lee opened the subject nearest to his heart. 'Dear, you know what I want to ask,' he said. 'Will you let me take you south with me before the snows? And will you let Father McGrath marry us before we start?'

'Oh, Lee — when?' she asked.

'Today, dearest.'

'Oh, not today, Lee!'

'Tomorrow, then? And we'll spend our honeymoon in the log house. Just for a day or two of happiness together before taking up the trail. I know it will always be your home, Joyce, and that we shall often come back here, now that the unhappiness of the past is over.'

'Wait, Lee!' Joyce was wrinkling her forehead in that manner that always distressed him so much. 'I want to ask you something. Have you really told me everything — from the time when I had my fall from the horse until I awakened in the forest with you? Or have you hidden something out of consideration for me?'

'Why do you ask that, dear?'

'Because I — I feel that you have, Lee.

I don't know why. It's just an instinct I have. And if there is something more, I should like to be told, because — because I have a feeling that it may help me to recover that part of my life that's still a blank to me.'

Lee felt in a quandary. It was impossible to wish to keep anything from Joyce; and yet he felt that she ought never to know the incidents of that day and night at Siston Lake.

'If you don't want to tell me, dear — ' Joyce went on.

Lee had to tell her then, and did, minimizing the affair in all but its essentials. He said nothing about his fight with the Free Traders, but told her how she had been kidnaped by the two men and taken to Rathway's camp, and how, in the absence of the band, he had rescued her.

'And you say I was unconscious all that time?' asked Joyce. 'I wish I could understand it, and I wish I could remember. It seems so strange that part of my memory should come back to me, and not all of it. Who were those men and what did they want of me? Were they Rathway's men? And what did he want?'

'I think the explanation is simple, dear,' Lee answered. 'Rathway wants the secret of your father's mine. In some way he must have learned that you were coming back to the range. He sent his men to intercept you. They probably told you that Rathway had your father in his power, and that's why you proposed to accompany them, and why you didn't want me.'

'Not want you, Lee? I wanted you from the first minute I saw you. I fell in love with you that evening in the hotel, and I've been in love with you ever since . . . But why was I riding in the range? What was it on my mind so terrible that there seems a sort of blackness there? I felt that you could save me,' She shook her head. 'No, there's more to it than that, my dear. And, I don't know . . . perhaps I shall never know.'

Lee slipped his arm about her. 'Don't try to think. It doesn't matter anymore. You're no longer the unknown woman traveling alone through a wilderness whose disappearance would arouse no suspicions. Once you're my wife, Rathway cannot harm you. And then you have Father McGrath behind you, and the church that he represents, and the missionary societies behind that. Rathway's not fool enough to buck a powerful organization by any crime — his cue is to lie low and sell all the liquor he can before we put him out of business. Tell me you'll marry me soon.'

'But the mine, Lee? And poor Leboeuf?'

'We'll look into those matters during our little honeymoon. Tell me that it shall be tomorrow.'

Joyce hesitated; and while she hesitated they heard the tinkle of bells, and Father McGrath appeared in his horse sleigh, coming up the hill. They went to the door. The jolly priest waved his hand and pulled in.

'Well, Mister Anderson, and so ye're back again!' he cried heartily, gripping Lee's hand with a fist of iron. ''Tis hard going with the horse through the snow, and I reckon I'll have to take to the dogs mighty soon. This is winter for sure at last!' He scrutinized the pair keenly. 'Ye havna made another of your quick changes?' he inquired, with an absurd affectation of archness that set them both laughing.

'No; I've fulfilled the conditions that were imposed on me,' Lee answered, and with that narrated his adventures in the mine. 'And Miss Pelly has promised to marry me tomorrow,' he ended mendaciously.

'N — not tomorrow, Lee,' said Joyce.

And Father McGrath, who had been listening to Lee's story with many frowns, looked so severe that Lee had a sudden fear that he would refuse to perform the ceremony.

'The day after, then, Joyce?' Lee pleaded.

Joyce interposed no veto this time, but was blushing like a rose and looking adorably confused.

'Well . . . ' began the father. 'Well, I'm not in favor of such quickness. Have you two young folks considered the consequences of matrimony, the awful and inevitable consequences? Have ye thought of the horror of sitting down opposite each other at the breakfast table mornin' after mornin' for the rest of your lives together? Have ye thought of the stunning responsibilities of the married state?'

Lee was beginning to grow alarmed, but suddenly he discerned a twinkle in the worthy father's eyes. And suddenly Father McGrath smote Lee violently upon the back.

'I'll do it, man!' he shouted. 'I'll do it. 'Tis the one practical joke that is permissible to a minister. I believe in matrimony. 'Tis the grandest of the dispensations of Our Lord on earth!' He paused and looked at them quizzically. Then: 'Well, we'll just say the day after tomorrow, Anderson,' he said. 'For ye ken, Anderson, a woman wants a little time to picture herself a bride in her mind's eye before she becomes one.'

14

The Best Laid Plans

Father McGrath had insisted that Lee should remain as a guest at the mission during the two following days, and he insisted on supplying him with an outfit of clothing. He asked their plans and Lee told him.

'The best thing in the world,' he said. 'Ye'll be safe at the house, and dinna have any fear of those devil's agents at Siston Lake, for they'll ken all about the pair of ye long since, and they darena interfere with ye now. But dinna prolong your honeymoon too long, for ye must be out of the range before the heavy snows begin.'

Lee and Father McGrath had a long talk together that night. Lee told him the whole story of his encounter with Joyce in the range, the dynamiting, and his pursuit of the band at Siston Lake, and rescue of her, culminating with their flight into the forest and Joyce's loss of memory.

At first the father listened and interrupted, and kept giving vent to exclamations of amazement and indignation; but as Lee went on with his story he fell into silence, puffing at his pipe beside the stove and looking at Lee intently.

''Tis amazing!' he said when Lee had ended. 'I canna understand it. For, look you, Anderson, it isna as if this was a country of savages, where a base man could do what he pleased. 'Tis true they sell their filthy hooch, but that's different from kidnaping women and attempting murder. There's something at the back of this that we havena hit upon.'

Next morning, Lee slept late — so late that it was the recitations of the school children across the open space that aroused him. From his bed he could hear Joyce's voice directing them, and he smiled happily at the thought of her. The morrow was his marriage day. The evening of the morrow they would be together in their log home, shut off from all the world. He dressed and strolled across the interval to the schoolhouse.

That was the happiest day of his life. Joyce, at his mandate, agreed to a half holiday, and all that afternoon they strolled through the snowbound woods, their arms about each other, planning their life together. Lee came more and more to see that to Joyce happiness consisted of the wilderness. She would wilt in a city. She had endured the period of her medical training only as a preliminary to returning to the wilds.

They decided that they would make their homes there, Lee resigning from the police the following spring. They would take up work under Father McGrath, enlarge the log house, create a garden; in time to come, settlers would flock in, the whisky traffic would go . . . They dreamed for hours until the advent of night sent them homeward.

The next afternoon, an old Indian and his wife were requisitioned for witnesses; and in the little schoolroom, in the presence of the entire population of the settlement, which consisted of the children, two half grown women, and a young boy, with an aged squaw or two — all legacies of the great smallpox epidemic of four years before which had decimated the region — Father McGrath performed the simple ceremony that united them, taking the gold ring from his own finger and handing it to Lee, who put it on his bride's. Lee, looking at Joyce with a new wonder that was almost fear, discovered the purpose that had sent him into the range. And in Joyce's confused and blushing face, in her eyes as she raised them shyly toward his own, he read their mutual happiness.

With Joyce's arm drawn shyly through his own, and his shoulders aching from Father McGrath's handclasp, he left the schoolhouse. Outside, the horse stood harnessed to the sleigh, which was loaded with the supplies. Lee handed Joyce inside and followed her. Father McGrath took the box seat of the big sleigh, which had originally functioned in the streets of some provincial city. He had driven it to his destination by a detour round the range, with all his worldly goods packed inside it.

The journey was a slow one, the horse slipping on the frozen snow and plunging through the crusts that had formed over the surface. It was even colder than before, and there seemed no doubt that winter had set in at last. All were glad when the log house came into view.

Father McGrath got down, flapping his arms. Lee helped Joyce out. They set down the supplies.

'I'll help you in with these goods,' said the priest, 'but I won't come inside. Goodbye and good luck to ye,' he added, extending a hand to each. But in the middle of that handclasp he stood still, listening. His face grew grim. Lee listened too. And at first he heard only the night wind stirring among the trees; then something more ominous, yet very faint, coming out of the distance.

It died away. The two men watched each other's faces with a surmise that did not find vent in utterance. Perhaps it had been the wind, the waves lapping the shore; but now it came again, louder and unmistakable. Lee dared not raise his eyes to meet Joyce's questioning gaze, lest she should discern the sudden fear.

For it was the put-putting of Rathway's motorboat.

The three might have been figures of stone as they stood there, listening to the sound of the engine, which grew rapidly louder. None of the three uttered a word.

Then the boat came into view, nearing the bank. It contained four men. One of them was Rathway. And even though Joyce was his inseparably, Lee waited for the sensation of an icy hand clutching his heart.

Father McGrath spoke. "'Tis Rathway, and I don't doubt but that he's some devil's work afoot. But hand steady, Anderson. He won't dare, he won't dare . . . '

His voice trailed off into silence. The engine of the motorboat had been shut off. Rathway and his men had stepped out. They were ashore; they were coming up from the river toward the house, Rathway a little in the lead of the others. With his hunched shoulders and his great muscular strength, his look of malignant, mocking ferocity, he seemed the nearest thing that Lee had known to incarnate evil.

His face as he drew near the group was twisted in a wry, triumphant smile. He looked mockingly at Lee. He looked ironically at Father McGrath. But there was possession anticipated in the look he cast at Joyce, and Lee drew her to his side, his arms about her, standing a little in front of her to protect her from the sight of Rathway.

Father McGrath stepped forward. 'Ye have no business here with my friends, James Rathway!' he cried. 'Ye ken very well the agreement we've entered into. So ye can take yersel' and your devil's crew away!'

'Aye?' sneered Rathway, regarding the priest with ironic banter. 'But I followed you and this party here because you weren't at the mission. It's not my plan to stay.'

'What do you want?' McGrath demanded.

'My wife,' Rathway returned, stretching

out his hand to place it on Joyce's shoulder.

With a loud cry, Joyce leaped back, staring about her as if she did not know where she was. Lee let his clenched fist fall. The situation was too big for physical retort.

'Ay, my wife. Father McGrath,' Rathway said again. 'Married to me two years ago in Montreal. And there's the certificate.' He held out a document.

Father McGrath's first words before looking at it were characteristic: ''Tis the first time I've heard of the man and not the woman keepin' the marriage lines, James Rathway.'

Lee was holding Joyce, who swayed in his arms. 'What does he mean?' he kept repeating. 'It's some trick. Tell them it's a trick, Joyce!'

But Joyce seemed neither to hear nor to understand anything. Meanwhile Father McGrath, who had been examining the paper, handed it back with an ironical bow.

'Miss Pelly was united in the bonds of holy matrimony with Mister Anderson here these three hours since,' he said. 'I'd take her word against your own and call that a forgery.' But the priest's face shone deathly white in the moonlight.

'Aye?' sneered Rathway, pointing a long finger at Joyce. 'Let her deny it, if she dares!'

Joyce said not a word. She lay in Lee's arms as if she had been mortally stricken. A deadly fear began to creep over Lee, over McGrath. Behind Rathway, Shorty and Pierre and a third man grinned and shifted uneasily.

'And that's a lie, anyhow,' said Father McGrath scornfully.

Rathway bowed sneeringly in turn. 'Permit me to go on. Father; believe or disbelieve, it makes no difference. He sent Joyce away to school to Montreal. Soon after, it was discovered that Pelly was wanted for an old murder — '

'Lie number two,' said the priest. ''Twas you who betrayed him — I have no doubt of that.'

'He fled the country,' pursued Rathway, unruffled. 'As his only friend, fearing that his daughter might come to harm in

Montreal, I went down there, saw her, and offered to make her my wife. She consented with alacrity — '

'Oh, aye, and we'll just cut out the alacrity,' said Father McGrath in abysmal disgust, 'because she didna, and if she did, it ill becomes you to say so.'

'She married me at the Church of the Virgin, as this certificate proves. And it was agreed that she should continue her mission studies for a certain period before coming to live with me as my wife. I proposed to build a comfortable home for her at Siston Lake and go into the fur business.'

'Fur?' shouted McGrath. 'The only fur you've ever traded in is what ye've put on the tongues and stomachs of your victims, ye cheap poison-peddlin' hooch-hound!'

Rathway went on as if he had not heard the insult. 'Last month, when she completed her course, she started north to meet me. As I was away on a business trip, I detailed two of my men to escort her from Little Falls. They met her. This man was with her, and he ordered them away under threat of shooting.'

He turned to Lee with a scowl. 'At Mrs. Rathway's urgent request, they went away to avoid bloodshed, but waited in the vicinity to make sure that no violence was offered her. As she did not reach their camping place, they became alarmed and went back. They found her lying under her horse, apparently abandoned by him after some accident — if it was only an accident.

'They brought her to Siston Lake, where I had just returned. This man followed them, attacked and stunned me from behind, stole a boat and two packs, and took her away, and appears to have been living a tramp's life in the woods with my wife ever since.'

Lee, who was still holding Joyce, started, but Father McGrath held up his hand. 'No, no, let him finish his lying story,' he said.

'That's all,' said Rathway. 'In spite of all, I'm willing to forgive the past and take her back. She was unconscious when this man got her into his power. He shall pay for what he's done, if there's law in this land — but this poor woman has been more sinned against than sinning. I'm willing to acknowledge her as my wife still. And I defy you, Father McGrath, to intervene.'

Father McGrath walked a step or two toward Joyce, who was standing, encircled by Lee's arm, her eyes cast down. She raised them to his face in mute appeal.

'My child, there's only one thing to ask of ye. Did you marry this man? Can ye remember?'

Joyce shuddered, and she looked at the priest hopelessly. 'Yes, it's true,' she answered. 'I married him.'

A cry broke from Lee's lips. He released Joyce, and stood looking at her with the expression of a man who has received his death blow.

'Yes, it's true,' said Joyce. She was speaking now with the calmness of one for whom nothing matters. 'He came to me with the threat that he had my father in his power and would betray him unless I married him. It had been the terror of my father's life for years that someday he'd be arrested for that old murder. And therefore — yes, I married him, but I insisted that I was to finish my course before I lived with him as his wife. Then, last month, he wrote to me that he would wait no longer. He said my father, who he'd helped to escape across the frontier, had returned to the district, and that he'd notify the authorities unless I came up to him immediately. And so I started, and — and God knows I could bear it no longer, and that's why he mercifully gave me forgetfulness!' Shuddering, she remained standing where she was like a cataleptic.

'So ye lied there, too!' cried Father McGrath to Rathway in white-hot wrath. 'Ye've proved yersel' a triple liar now, for Pelly's dead.'

'Dead?' shouted Rathway.

'Aye, dead these many months, and ye claimed he was alive, and in your power, so that ye could get possession of this poor woman ye've deceived.'

But he broke off, and Rathway made no reply, but watched him as he strode to the spot where Joyce was standing. Gently he took her hand in his and began to whisper in her ear. And all the while there was silence, and yet it seemed as if through that silence, innumerable powers were in conflict — man against man, man against law, man against God.

Then Lee cried out in a tone so wild that even Rathway and his men appeared awed by it: 'She's mine in the sight of God! Joyce, tell me that you care nothing for this trick that's been played on you! Tell me that you'll defy this man and come away with me!'

Rathway stepped forward, covering Lee with a pistol. 'By heaven,' he swore, 'I'll blow your brains out if you meddle with me or mine, and there's no court in this land will hold me guilty.'

Lee scarcely seemed to be aware of him. He was holding out his arms to Joyce, and she was trembling, and looking at him, irresolute. Father McGrath was holding her hands and still whispering in her ear. And suddenly a dreadful change came over Lee's face. Confidence was replaced by a look of mortal anguish.

'Joyce!' he cried wildly.

Joyce looked at the priest, who stepped between them; but it was Joyce who he addressed, not Lee.

'My child, you married James Rathway of your own free will,' he said. 'The motive has no bearing on the situation. He didna constrain you by fear of violence. 'Twas to save your father you did it, you say — aye, but 'twas to save him from the just processes of the law. There's no way out, my dear. This man's your husband.' He looked at Lee. ''Tis the saddest thing I've known,' he said, 'but ye see this makes the ceremony ye've been through valueless. There's no way out of it — none at all, lad. So you two must just say goodbye.'

Lee turned to Joyce. He cried her name. She tottered toward him, hands outstretched, groping before her, as if she were blind.

She found him, their hands clasped each other thus during a period of silence that seemed all eternity compressed into a few moments. The words came monotonously from Lee's lips: 'Joyce, are you — going — to that man who calls himself your husband?'

She bowed her head. Their eyes met,

his in a dumb prolongation of that question, hers in mute, helpless agony.

Then suddenly Lee released her. He straightened himself, stood up stiffly, and squared his shoulders as if he were on parade. And quietly he turned away.

Then the silence was broken by a wild laugh from Rathway. There was something in that laugh more devilish even than in the situation. For it was amused, shameless, merciless, devoid of any human element; it was like the laugh that the hyena gives over the kiss of some nobler beast that it has supplanted.

'Put his pack out of my house, Pierre! Fling it out into the snow!' he shouted, chuckling. 'What, your pack, is it? Never mind, we'll let him keep it. Can't turn the poor devil out into the snow to freeze. He'll go to jail later on for *stealing* it.'

He strode up to Joyce and clapped his hand upon her shoulder. 'Joyce, my dearie, have you said goodbye to your sweetheart?' he asked. 'We'll make this place our headquarters for a little honeymoon before going back to Siston Lake — what d'you say to that?'

She shrank under his touch. Rathway saw it and scowled. But he turned toward Lee, his face alight with triumph.

'You — take yourself away with your stolen goods, and don't let me catch you hanging round my wife again!' he shouted. 'Or I'll shoot you like the dog that you are. And harken, Mr. Anderson! Don't you ever dare to show your face among decent men again, or I'll have you jailed!'

Father McGrath strode forward, his face working with emotion. 'Aye, James Rathway, ye're feeling your triumph now,' he cried, 'and the yellow cur's come to the top in ye. But ye'll remember that there's a higher power sometimes makes hash of even the best laid plans!'

Then he strode to where Lee was standing, and clapped his hand on his shoulder. 'Will ye no come back to the mission with me this night, Mister Anderson?' he pleaded.

But Lee stood like a stone, appearing not to be conscious of the priest's question, while Rathway, with an evil smile, put his arm round Joyce's waist and led her, nonresistant, toward the log house, followed by his three aides.

And to McGrath that was the most awful moment in his whole career, and all the manhood in him urged him to fight, fight to the death against this human sacrifice. It was only his lifetime of discipline that held him at Lee's side. And, looking into Lee's stony face, an immense pity swelled up in his heart.

The door of the hut closed. Lee quivered and started as the priest's hand fell on his shoulder again.

'Lee, lad, ye'll come back with me,' Father McGrath pleaded.

An inarticulate sound like that of some animal broke from Lee's lips. And, shaking himself free from the priest's friendly grasp, he picked up the rifle and the snow shoes, and went slouching off in the direction of the forest. Father McGrath took a step or two toward him, then, abating his head, watched him as he made his way over the frozen ground into the darkness.

Sighing, the priest turned back to the sleigh. He gathered up the reins; then with an impulse of sudden fury, shook his fist toward the log house, lying peacefully enough in the bosom of the frozen valley, bathed in moonlight.

'If I weren't a priest of God, and believe that He brings all things right in His good time accordin' to His will, I'd throttle ye like the hound ye are!' he cried.

15

Joyce Fights a Good Fight

Joyce let Rathway lead her inside the log house without offering any resistance. She moved like an automaton under the pressure of his arm. Inside the large room, he released her.

'Put down my pack!' he ordered Shorty, who was attending him. 'Light some candles and pin something over the window, and then get out!'

In a minute, Rathway and Joyce were alone. She shuddered as the candlelight revealed Rathway's face to her. She had seen it so many times in fearful dreams, and all the way up through the range. When she had married Rathway, she had hoped against hope that something would intervene to save her; but now the blow had fallen. And she stood quite still, her hands crossed on her breast, waiting for what was to come.

Then Rathway seized her in his arms. He kissed her ice-cold lips, cheeks, eyes, and throat. His hands went pawing over her. And as she still stood nonresistant and unresponsive, his passion grew the fiercer, and mingled with fury at the realization that this woman, so submissive in his arms, was his in body alone.

He released her, and in his rage began to growl out jeers and curses. 'A *different* honeymoon from what you were expecting, Joyce!' he cried. 'No, no, the *same* honeymoon, but a different husband. A better one, eh? Well, can't you speak? Which of your two men do you prefer?'

But Joyce made no reply.

'You've answered me, you drab!' Rathway shouted. 'So you've been *living with him* on the trail these two weeks past! By heaven, I was a fool to take you back from him without killing him! You thought I'd swallow that lie about your having forgotten you were a married woman, did you? Did you ever hear of a woman *forgetting* that she was married?'

Joyce only watched him with a fixed gaze that made him uneasy.

'You won't pretend to me that your relations with him were *innocent*, I suppose?'

Still Joyce said nothing, and Rathway grasped her by the wrists.

'Answer me! Were they?'

'Yes, they were innocent.' The words issued mechanically from her lips. He glared at her, incredulous, wanting to he convinced, unable to be. Of course she was lying. He would rather have known the worst than remain in that state of uncertainty. He didn't understand her. It was barely possible, no more. He was choking at the sight of her — his, yet in spirit a world away. And suddenly he fell upon his knees, seized her hands, and began impressing kisses upon them.

'Forgive me!' he stammered. 'I'm mad with jealousy. I know you were unconscious and at his mercy when he took you away. You weren't to blame. I love you, Joyce. I've always been mad about you, you know that. Once, when I lost my head, your father shot me. Won't you forget this other man, this Anderson? He means no good to you. He's after that mine, no doubt, and that's why he forced his company upon you in the range. Forget him, Joyce. I love you. I'll make you a good husband, and you shall be a rich woman. We'll give up this life here and go south, where people know how to live. Can you love me, Joyce?'

'No,' she answered. 'I don't love you. I've always hated you.'

'By heaven, I'll show you!'

He was hoarse with passion. But as he tried to seize her in his arms again, she drew away suddenly, stopped — and then he saw that she had a hunting knife in her hand.

'Listen to me now, James Rathway,' she said, still speaking in the same strained, monotonous tone. 'I shall never be yours. I shall kill myself first. I would have fulfilled my compact in the spirit and the letter, had you fulfilled yours. But I didn't trust you. I suspected that you were tricking me — as you were.'

'That's a lie. I didn't trick you. Put down that knife!'

'It's not a lie. You tricked me twice. The first time, you forced me into a marriage with you by the threat that unless I consented you'd betray my father to the police. I married you, and *still* you betrayed him.'

'I did not. Someone else must have done so. Why should I have betrayed him? He was my friend.'

'You were the only man who knew his secret. Then the second time, knowing that I'd never live with you, you sent me a lying message to lure me up here, saying that you held my father in your power. You knew that nothing else on earth would bring me up to you. And it was a *lie*, because my father's been dead for months past.'

Rathway's face blanched. 'I don't believe that story. How do you know?'

'He died in his mine. His body lies at the bottom of it, where he was stricken. If you didn't know that he was dead, at least you were lying when you said he was in your power.'

'He lies — at the bottom — the bottom of the mine?' Rathway stammered. 'I — I didn't know.' He seemed to shake off a sort of stupor. He tried to take her hand.

'Joyce, if I did lie to you, it was only because I love you. God, think of the years I've loved you! I've given all my life to the hope of winning you. Isn't a woman touched by the thought of that? All that I've ever done, since that day when I first saw you in your father's house, has been for you. And now I've got you, and you tell me you will never — '

He was pressing toward her, but she held the dagger pointed at him, and he stopped, afraid of the look in her eyes. 'Don't be foolish. Put that knife away. What do you mean to do?'

'Kill you and then myself, if you lay a hand on me again. I've told you I shall never live with you.'

'By heaven, I'll kill him if you go to him!'

'I shall not go to him; that's why I sent him away. I shall go away alone.'

'Joyce, listen to sense. Do you realize that you're my wife? That I can hold you by force, and there's no law in the dominion to prohibit me, and no man who would not approve? Joyce, be sensible. If you're still in love with this man, Anderson, I'm willing to wait till you've forgotten him a little. Lord, I've waited long enough for you! But I'll wait longer if I have to. Don't you see how foolishly you're acting,' he pleaded. 'Don't you realize how much better off you're going to be with a husband who's rich and devoted to you? Your father never took a penny out of that mine all these years. There must be a hundred thousand dollars' worth of gold dust there — perhaps a million. Can't you see the old boy working night after night like a beaver, to make you and me rich?'

He threw back his head and uttered his hyena laugh again. But Joyce said nothing at all, and he added: 'I suppose you know it all belongs to me, as your husband, under the law, and that if you leave me you don't get a penny of it?'

'Well?'

'Well? I thought you mightn't understand. How far from here is the mine?'

'I don't know.'

He burst into a spasm of fury. 'By heaven, I'm going to make you know! Do you think you're going to keep the secret of my own mine from me? I tell you I meant to have it from the first moment that your father began dropping his hints, the old fool. It was to find out about it that I stayed on with him year after year.'

'I've always known that.'

Rathway stared at her. He was staggered by the quiet, indifferent manner of her speaking. He had not believed her before. He had been so confident when he sent for her, under the pretext of having her father at his mercy, that she could solve the secret which he had never been able to solve himself. Yet now it began to occur to him as a probability that Joyce had never known the secret. He had taken too much for granted. If she had not known it when she went south, as had certainly been the case, how could she have learned it since? All his plans seemed suddenly defeated.

'You say you don't know where the mine is? Ah, but you told me your father's lying at the bottom of it!' he cried suddenly. 'Who found him there?'

'Mr. Anderson.'

'He knows, then? Your lover knows and

your husband doesn't? D'you mean to say it wasn't you who told him?'

'I've told him nothing, because I know nothing. He found the mine and found my father's body there. He hasn't told the secret to me, and I don't want to know.'

An extraordinary look came over Rathway's face, the look of the fox, the wolverine. He seemed to reflect — and suddenly he pounced. In an instant he had gripped Joyce by the arms, imprisoning the hand that held the knife. With a laugh he tore the hand open, took out the knife, and thrust it into his belt. He strained her against him.

'I've had enough of this nonsense, my dearie!' he cried triumphantly. 'You're going to make that lover of yours tell you the secret of the mine. You'll do it when you've learned to love me. And, by heaven, I'm going to make you!'

She screamed and beat furiously at his face, impotent in his grasp. They wrestled to and fro. So violent was her resistance that for a moment or two she held Rathway at bay, beating her fists in his face again and again, and drawing blood from his nose and lips.

The fury of her resistance only made her the more desirable in his eyes. He held her fast now, her arms forced to her sides again, his bloodshot eyes leering into hers, his black beard sweeping her cheek.

In the room they had taken at the rear of the house, the three men, who were drinking and playing cards, hearing Joyce's screams and the sounds of the struggle, burst into mirth, and came tiptoeing along the passage.

Joyce, making one final desperate effort, broke once more out of Rathway's arms, burst through the door, and ran screaming along the passage. She got the front door open.

'Lee! *Lee!* Come to me!' she cried in wild abandonment.

Then Rathway's arms closed about her from behind, and Joyce ceased to struggle.

16

Joyce or a Gold Mine

Lee did not go as far as the forest, which loomed out of the distance beyond the ridges of broken ground. He waited some little distance away, until the priest's sleigh had gone. Then he went quietly back toward the log house.

Lights burned inside. A strip of cloth had been pinned before the window of the largest room — the one in which he had camped with Joyce for a brief hour upon that afternoon of their arrival. This was the room that he had selected in his mind for their occupancy during their brief honeymoon.

But not the least spasm twisted Lee's face at the realization that *another* had supplanted him in that relationship with Joyce. There are some phases of emotion so tense that they appear to neutralize themselves by destroying their own manifestations.

Lee's expression showed not the smallest deviation from the normal now. It was quiet, dispassionate, and very cold. Softly he approached the window and, stooping, looked between the frame and the curtain of cloth. The window on this side had a piece missing out of the corner, and over the little gap someone had pasted a piece of paper. With the barrel of his rifle, Lee quietly made a small hole in it.

From there he could catch glimpses of the two figures. He heard their voices. He was in no hurry. He was waiting till they chose to finish their conversation. Then, in due time, Rathway would stand in a line with his sights and he would make an end of him.

The wild turmoil in Lee's heart seemed divorced from his brain, which remained impassive and cold and steady as the piece of mechanism in his hands.

Rathway's voice grew louder. Lee saw the hunched figure gesticulating, the sneer on his face. Lee drew a bead. He might as well end the business after all.

But before his finger tightened on the trigger, a hand upon his shoulder made him leap to his feet and start up, his rifle clubbed, ready to strike. He thought Rathway's men had surprised him.

But to his amazement, it was a woman standing at his side; then in that cloaked and hooded figure that confronted him, he recognized — Estelle once more.

She looked at him fixedly; she was deeply agitated, and caught at her breath before she was able to find her voice.

'You fool!' she exclaimed bitterly. 'You fool! You had her in your hands and you let Jim Rathway take her away from you! You couldn't hold her — and now I come upon you to find you planning a cold-blooded, cowardly murder — *you*, a policeman!'

At that, something broke in Lee's heart. The realization of the act he planned came over him. He would have killed Rathway as heedlessly as any bloodthirsty forest beast. But Estelle's reference to the police touched his pride. He let the rifle drop, grounding the butt.

'Listen to what I've got to tell you, Lee.

I love him. Do you understand that? I suppose you think it's not my nature to love. But it is! It was you who couldn't hold my love. I hated and despised you. I never knew how much I loved James Rathway till I found out how much I hated you that morning when you came to our camp and struck him down so treacherously. Oh, yes, I have love and passion, and constancy in my nature, Lee Anderson. It was only you who couldn't draw them out!' Her voice was vibrant, hoarse with passion. 'That woman will make a fool of you, too, Lee Anderson, just as I did,' she cried. 'You'd be made a fool of anywhere, by any woman!'

But her words passed Lee by like the wind.

'I could have killed you that morning, as I could kill you now, only — I love James Rathway. And he'll love me again when you take this new attraction away out of his sight, where he can't find her. I thought you'd got away — but here you are, back again with her, and all the work's got to be done over again.

'I was crouching near, and I overheard

your dialogue, you and she, and the priest, and James Rathway. You gave her up — the woman you love — because she'd stood up before the altar with the man she hated and called herself his wife. I'd hold the woman I loved, were I a man, against God himself, and all His cohorts!

'Oh, if only I could find words to hurt you, Lee Anderson, to pierce that tough skin of yours! But I haven't time. Listen to me, now! You don't have to commit murder to get her. You blind fool, shall I tell you how?' She laughed with taunting menace.

And suddenly came the sound of Joyce, screaming within the house. There came the noise of a struggle. Even as Lee turned, Joyce was running along the passage toward the door. Instantly Estelle glided away into the shadows.

Joyce flung the door open; and then Rathway caught her from behind and swung her back toward him. His black beard hung over her face.

'Lee! *Lee!* Come to me!'

Joyce ceased to struggle.

'Here!' answered Lee, and dashed his

fists into Rathway's face, sending him staggering.

Rathway howled and felt for his pistol. Lee was upon him, pinioning his arms to his sides, before he could draw it. But Rathway's men came hurrying along the passage. In an instant there was a furious melee. Lee tripped over a leg thrust out, fell heavily upon his back, and struggled in vain under the weight of his four adversaries. Quickly he was reduced to helplessness, his limbs held firmly. Momentarily he ceased to struggle, nursing his strength for a more violent effort. He looked up into the grinning faces, at Rathway, standing over him, leering, arms outstretched, gasping for breath and consciousness.

Rathway pulled his pistol and covered Lee. 'Pierre! Shorty! Kramer! You're witnesses that you saw this man spying outside this house.'

They assented. Pierre grinned. Shorty swore, spat, and scowled, and Lee saw the half-healed scar of his pistol butt upon his cheek.

'You saw him assault me,' Rathway

continued. 'Well, Anderson, I guess if I choose to shoot you like the dog you are, the law wouldn't have much to say about it. But I'll be reasonable. Get back to your quarters!' he snarled to his aides, and the three men, in surprise, released Lee and went down the passage.

Lee leaped to his feet, confronting Rathway resolutely, but puzzled. Rathway held him covered.

'You must want *my wife* mighty bad to come back like a fox at night in the hope of picking her up under my nose, Anderson,' said Rathway. 'Well, I'm a businessman, and I guess anyone can get most anything he wants if he wants it bad enough to be willing to pay the price for it. Maybe you can get her at the price, Anderson.

'Pelly's gold mine belongs to me under the law. She tells me you've found it and are holding the secret of it. All right. The price is Pelly's gold mine. Joyce for the mine. What d'you say to that, Anderson?' Rathway was trembling with eagerness. 'I was willing to overlook the past and take her back, but if she doesn't want me and does want you, I guess I can't hold her against her will. So I'm ready to take my mine instead and close the bargain. What d'you say to it, Anderson?'

Lee suspected some trick, but the anxiety on Rathway's face, the trembling tones of his voice showed that his avarice was a stronger passion than that for Joyce. And, despite the vileness of the proposal, Lee realized that in no other way could Joyce be saved. He knew that even then Rathway was contemplating treachery, but there was nothing else to do. If he refused, Rathway would shoot him in cold blood — and the law would justify him.

'I must speak to Miss Pelly first.'

'There's no Miss Pelly here,' Rathway snarled. 'If you mean Mrs. Rathway, you can have five minutes' talk with her to make up your mind. And if you don't accept, or try any tricks on me, by heaven, it's your last minute!'

Lee nodded, took Joyce by the arm, and drew her inside the room. Rathway stood in the doorway, covering him with his pistol, but Lee quietly closed the door on him, and Rathway accepted the situation. Lee went back to Joyce.

'Joyce! Joyce, darling!'

'Oh, Lee. I can't bear it. I thought I could, but it's impossible. Oh, take me away, Lee! Help me now, as you offered to help me on the range, though we can never be anything to each other. Take me somewhere to safety, where I need never see that man again, or think of him, or of this place, or — or ever remember anything of the past.'

She clung to him, sobbing in terror and loneliness. Lee, holding her, pressed her hands to his lips.

'Joyce, dearest. I'll do as he proposes, then. I'll show him the mine, and then I'll take you away somewhere south, where you need never think of him or of this place again. And if that wretched marriage can't be annulled, I'll be contented to be your brother for the rest of our lives, dear.'

He flung the door open. Rathway was standing uneasily behind it, and Lee felt pretty sure that he had been trying to listen with his ear to the ill-fitting jamb.

'I've decided to accept your proposition, Rathway,' said Lee. 'The terms are these: I guarantee nothing as to the mine; merely to conduct you to the place where Pelly worked for gold. I'll show you the secret entrance. This lady will accompany us, and you will leave your men behind. And we'll go unarmed.'

'But I shall carry Mr. Anderson's pistol,' Joyce interposed calmly, 'and I shall see that the terms are fairly carried out.'

Rathway shot a look of hatred at her. 'I've no objection to that either,' he answered, shrugging his shoulders nonchalantly.

'At sunrise, then — ' Lee began.

'At sunrise? God, man, do you suppose I'm going to wait till sunrise?' shouted Rathway. He took off his belt containing his pistol, and laid it on the floor. 'We'll start at once.'

Lee handed Joyce his pistol, then going into the room, extinguished the candle, brought it out, and slipped it into his pocket, and the three set out immediately. When they reached the rocking stone,

Lee looked back, scanning the country carefully in case Rathway's aides were following them.

He had expected treachery, but it was quite impossible for any spy to approach near enough to discover the entrance under the stone without being observed, as Rathway had himself discovered during his years of fruitless effort to follow old Pelly; and there was no sign of the three. It occurred to Lee that Rathway was not likely to wish the entrance to the mine to be known to any of his aides.

Rathway was looking uneasily about him. 'It's in the gorge, then?' he muttered. And, throwing off all pretense of concealment, 'There's no way down. I've walked round and round the damned place a thousand times.'

Lee tilted back the stone and showed Rathway the hole beneath it. Rathway stared at it in amazement, uttering an oath as the stone came back into position.

'I shall go first,' Lee said, 'and light the candle. Miss Pelly, will please follow me? You, Rathway, will come last.'

Lee pushed the stone back, lay down

on the ground, and, after showing Joyce how to elevate it from beneath, descended. When his feet were on the first rung of the ladder, he lit the candle. In a moment Joyce appeared, and then Rathway behind her, clinging to the opening and looking down with uneasy suspicion.

'Hold tight to the rocks,' Lee called. 'It's slippery, and if you lose your hold there's a deadly drop below.'

He led the way down, shifting the candle from hand to hand alternately as he descended, to illuminate the way for Joyce, until he reached the bottom orifice. Then he began slowly to complete the descent, instructing Joyce where to put her hands and feet, guiding her, and bracing himself against the cliff, ready to sustain her weight in case of a slip. However, all three reached the floor of the gorge without accident.

Rathway muttered, looking about him. In the moonlight, Lee saw that he was dripping with perspiration and trembling with excitement.

Lee said eight fatal words: 'The rock

marks the entrance to the tunnel.'

Rathway looked at it and nodded.

'I had some difficulty in finding it before,' Lee added. He turned to Joyce. 'Joyce dear, I'm going to show Rathway something that I think it would be better for you not to see. Will you wait where you are for a few minutes? We won't go out of your sight.'

'Very well, Lee,' the woman answered quietly. She had understood what Lee meant immediately. Lee took Rathway through the laurel tangles and showed him Pelly's remains. He showed him the initials on the handle of the revolver.

Rathway stood dumbly staring at the skeleton. He was trembling even more violently than before.

'He must have fallen from the cliff,' said Lee, indicating the broken bones.

'Aye, but where's your proof that it's Pelly?' Rathway burst out suddenly. 'Why, man, there isn't a court in the land would admit that skeleton as proof that Pelly was dead. That's as like as not the body of his Indian, carrying Pelly's revolver.'

Lee obeyed the instinct not to tell Rathway that Leboeuf was alive.

'Besides,' Rathway went on, 'as for C.P., well, that might mean anything. Charles Patrick or Clarence Peel. There used to be a Clarence Peel in this district who disappeared. I swear that's the truth, Anderson. Any old-timer will tell you that I'm not lying to you. N-no, Anderson, you can't prove that's the body of old Pelly, just from those initials.'

Lee wondered at Rathway's agitation. The man seemed quite beside himself. He twined his fingers in his black heard; had shambled away with his peculiar hunched slouch. Lee led him to the cross above the little grave.

'I think that's proof,' he said quietly.

But Rathway, clenching and unclenching his fists, said nothing. Lee went back, calling Joyce, and they proceeded in the direction of the cave. Lee pointed out the pans and cradle, and the proofs of dynamiting.

'Aye, but the gold — where's the gold?' Rathway demanded.

'I've seen none,' answered Lee, 'and, if

you remember, I made no guarantee as to it.'

'How do I know you haven't taken it away?' Rathway shouted. 'Aye, you may have stolen my gold as you stole my wife. You may be planning to take my wife and my gold away together.'

Lee looked at him in amazement, for Rathway was nearly crazed by some passion. Probably, Lee thought, the anticipation of obtaining the treasure of old Pelly.

'I've taken no gold and I've seen none,' he answered. 'I must again remind you of our agreement, Rathway.'

Rathway pulled himself together with an effort. 'Aye, that's all right,' he answered. 'This looks like Pelly's mine. Let's look inside. Have you been inside, Anderson?'

'I've only explored the entrance,' Lee answered. 'I brought no candle with me last time I was here.'

Relighting the candle, he preceded Rathway within. The sound of the distant roaring came immediately to their ears. By the candle light, Lee saw fresh footprints on the sands. They had been made by a man wearing moccasins, no doubt Leboeuf. He did not call Rathway's attention to them, and Rathway, absorbed with his eagerness to find the treasure, noticed nothing. Lee wondered, however, what the Indian had been doing in the cavern.

The cave grew narrower; then, just when Lee thought that they had reached the end, it suddenly vaulted out and up into a large chamber. The roaring of the waterfall immediately became accentuated as the sounds echoed from wall to wall. By the light of the candle, they could now see what looked like a sheer drop into darkness immediately in front of them.

They drew back from the edge hastily. But the next moment they perceived that what they had taken for a precipice was a river. Inky black, a swift and perfectly soundless stream rushing through the cavern from side to side of the mountain.

It emerged through a low tunnel in the rock and disappeared through another, barely two feet in height, upon the other side. And the roaring that they heard was not caused by this stream within the cave, but by some distant cataract, either beyond the mountain or deep within the bowels of the earth.

There were evidences, in the shape of rusty pots and kettles, and disintegrating tins strewn about the place, that this had been Pelly's headquarters, while on the opposite side of the cavern there was a deep sand tunnel extending into a smaller cavern under the wall, showing that Pelly had worked this part for gold. The whole interior was piled high with wood ashes and remains of charred logs. This seemed, in fact, to be the heart of Pelly's gold mine.

Suddenly Rathway, who had been wandering apparently aimlessly about the interior, uttered a shout and leaped toward the obscurity of the opposite wall. In another moment he had returned, dragging with him a large sack. As if unconscious of the presence of Lee and Joyce, he kneeled down, and muttering feverishly, begun untying the cord about the sack's mouth. The gaping sides disclosed a pit of gold. Gold in fine dust, gold in nuggets.

Rathway plunged his arms within the sack up to the elbows, chuckling and mumbling. There was a fortune in that bag, the accumulation of old Pelly's years of nocturnal labors. It was impossible to estimate it, but it would make its possessor a very rich man for life.

'Well, I'm glad you've got it,' said Lee. But he was thinking bitterly of Joyce's loss.

He turned away. Suddenly some instinct caused him to duck and spin around. The flash of flame spurted almost into his face. He heard Joyce's cry ring through the cavern.

Rathway had pulled a second pistol from his clothes and fired at Lee at a distance of five or six feet. The bullet chipped a sliver of granite from the wall behind his head. At the same instant, Lee saw Joyce aim her automatic and fire deliberately at Rathway.

But of course no discharge followed the pulling of the trigger. Lee had known the automatic was empty, though it had not seemed necessary to warn her.

As he sprung forward, Rathway brought the butt of the weapon smashing down upon Lee's forehead. Lee dropped foolishly upon his knees; he saw Rathway's face, convulsed with fury, over him; Rathway's arm, yellow with gold dust, raised to strike again. Lee leaned backward, overbalanced, fell into the stream.

He saw Joyce run forward and grasp at him as he was swept past, saw Rathway grappling with her — then he was in the whirling current, and Joyce and Rathway and the cavern vanished as swiftly as a picture on the screen.

Lee was only dimly conscious of what was happening to him, for his senses reeled under Rathway's blow, and it was only an intense effort of the will that enabled him to keep his face above the water. He had a vague consciousness that he was being whirled through the depths of the mountain in complete darkness. The rock roof swept his hair, and the rock walls on his two sides formed a sort of hydraulic tube against which the stream tossed and buffeted him, hurling him from side to side in its fury. And ever the stream grew swifter, and ever that ominous roaring sounded louder in his ears.

The river was carrying him toward some subterranean waterfall. Half conscious, Lee visualized death among the grinding rocks — death in that viscous blackness that no ray of sunlight had ever illuminated. He knew in a dim way that this was the end, and resistance being impossible, resigned himself to the rush of the waters, gasping in a few mouthfuls of air whenever it was possible.

The tunnel was growing still narrower, and now the roaring sounded in his ears like thunder. The rock roof dipped to the water. Lee drew in one last breath. He went under. He flung up his arms, and his fingers scraped the roof — then touched only emptiness. The current hurled him to the surface again. He opened his eyes.

Starlight overhead, appearing between high, precipitous walls, that seemed to scrape the sky; a narrow gorge, through which the current whirled him still more furiously. In the distance, a line of white — the boiling of the torrent about the rocks of the falls.

Involuntarily a great cry of anguish broke from Lee's throat. Again and again it broke forth, the spontaneous protest of the body against inevitable destruction.

Upon the brink of the gorge, which had a tiny ledge of rock or undercliff beside the water, a beacon fire leaped into view far away. Silhouetted against it was the black figure of a man. Lee fancied that he shouted in answer. His head was growing clearer now.

The gorge had become as narrow as a hall bedroom, and the rush of the black torrent toward the falls terrific. It whirled Lee around and around like a ball. The line of white was coming nearer with awful rapidity. Lee saw the figure on the edge of it, tossing its arms as it raced along the brink, but if it was shouting now, its voice was indistinguishable in the roar of the torrent.

Great fallen rocks lined the banks. Lee grasped at them as he was swept by, but they always eluded him, always the current carried him away. Now he seemed poised upon the brink of the tumbling cataract. He grasped at a rock projecting out of midstream, missed it . . .

Something descended over his head, checking him. He seemed to float still in the current, which boiled about and past him. He reached out to the rock, found it, clung there. He reached up one arm and found that he was enveloped in the folds of a long fishing net. He saw Leboeuf upon the brink, not ten feet distant. The man was shouting, but Lee could not distinguish a word. He was pointing toward the shore, to the rock. Lee let himself go.

The great shoulders and arms strained themselves upon the net against the torrent. Completely enmeshed, Lee felt himself being slowly drawn like a gigantic fish toward the bank. There was one instant when the force of the current seemed to be pulling old Leboeuf into the stream. The huge body bent like a bow, there was an instant of suspense, then slowly the great shoulders swung back, and Lee grasped the rocky ledge through the folds of the net. He felt himself raised to the rock rim, felt Leboeuf's arms about him, and collapsed into unconsciousness.

17

Rathway Takes Thought of His Spoils

Rathway laughed like a hyena as he saw Lee disappear in the swift waters of the torrent. He spun about and struck the pistol from Joyce's hands, pulled her to him, and crushed her brutally against his breast. And Joyce, overcome by this climax of the night's work, suddenly relaxed in his arms and fainted.

Rathway laid her down on the sand and looked at her in perplexity. He discovered that he was somewhat in the same situation as the fox with the sack of corn and the goose. If he carried Joyce through the tunnel and left her while he went back for the gold, she might escape him. On the other hand, if he left her in the cave while he carried the gold away, she might fling herself into the stream in her despair. And someone might take the gold.

The only thing for Rathway to do was to remove the gold and Joyce simultaneously. He carried the bag of gold to the cave mouth, but in spite of his great strength, the weight was terrific. He reconciled himself to his labors, however, by the reflection that the bag contained a fortune.

Then, returning to Joyce, he carried her to the bag and set her down beside it. It was fortunate for him that she remained unconscious, or he would have been impossibly handicapped in his maneuvers. Cursing and struggling, first with the bag and then with the woman, Rathway at last got them to the rock at the foot of the tunnel which Lee had so indiscreetly pointed out to him.

Then arose the most difficult problem of all. Either Joyce or the gold would have to be left on the upper side of the tunnel while he went back for the other. And during his absence, Rathway shuddered at the thought of any prowler coming along and making off with the treasure. He was not convinced in his mind that his aides had not followed him.

Rathway chose to leave the gold in safety. It was the greater of his two passions. Gathering Joyce in his arms, he essayed the ascent of the cliff.

How he got to the tunnel's entrance he hardly knew afterward. It was a feat which only the spur of triumph enabled him to accomplish. He had to hold on with both hands while gripping Joyce with the insides of his arms. At length, however, he did succeed in reaching the tunnel's mouth, dragging himself through, and pulling Joyce through after him. The ascent of the rock ladder was trifling in comparison.

He looked at Joyce. She was still in a condition of profound unconsciousness. Breathing an unvoiced prayer to whatever gods controlled his soul that she would not awake, Rathway laid her down between the monolith and the rocking stone, and went back for the gold.

This job of hoisting the heavy bag up the side of the cliff required less dexterity, but every ounce of strength that he possessed. Inch by inch, straining and scrambling up the rocky wall, Rathway pushed it before him until, bruised by the impact of the treasure, he got it safely within the tunnel, and thence to the rocking stone above.

He stopped to breathe. He wiped the sweat from his face. It was not very far from dawn. He must have spent hours on that hideous task.

Then, carrying the bag and the woman alternately, he pushed on toward the house. He wakened his aides with a bellow. They came staggering out, drunk and half asleep.

'Start up the engine, Kramer,' he shouted. 'We'll have to be on our way by daylight. Gimme a drink!' He gulped down half a bottle of his own liquor. The reaction after his incredible labors, the possession of the gold; the supreme triumph of that night exalted him. But he was anxious to get away as soon as possible. At Siston Lake, which was only a few hours' journey by motorboat, he would be in his own retreat. He could wait till then to enjoy success. He gloated as he looked down at the unconscious Joyce.

Something had gone wrong with the engine, and Rathway fussed and fumed while Kramer, the mechanic, was repairing it. The packs were got together, the engine overhauled. Rathway placed the bag of gold dust in the middle of the boat and carried Joyce to it. He laid her down, and they pushed off.

Joyce had fallen into a profound sleep of exhaustion. She began to stir, stretching out her arms. 'Lee, dear,' she murmured. She opened her eyes and looked into Rathway's vulpine face.

She screamed. She struggled. She remembered.

She fought like a madwoman, and Rathway was forced to call for a rope. He tied her ankles together and fastened her arms to her sides, and passed the rope around one of the cleats. In spite of her bonds, she struggled so that it was all Rathway could do to keep her from tilting the boat over. She screamed continually and tried to throw herself over the side.

At last she stopped, however, and lay still from exhaustion. She never renewed her struggles. She lay at the bottom of the boat with her eyes closed, drawing in convulsive breaths. Despite his triumph and his anticipations, Rathway was afraid of her. He wondered what was going on inside her mind.

It was about noon when they reached the promontory. Rathway, preceded by Pierre and Shorty with the gold — he would not leave it in the motorboat — carried Joyce across the neck of land to an isolated hut about three hundred yards away, following a secret passage among the reeds. He laid her down upon the camp bed. Joyce lay rigid, looking at him with diluted pupils and still drawing in those shuddering breaths. Rathway went out with a sigh of relief; he was still more afraid of her in that condition.

Another person he feared was Estelle, and it was with relief he learned that she was not at the promontory. Estelle had odd ways of wandering alone about the country. Rathway was glad of this temporary respite. Going to the stables, a shanty with two stalls close by where he kept two horses and fodder for use in unexpected emergency, he saw that one of the animals was missing. No doubt Estelle had gone out riding.

Estelle's personality was a stronger one than Rathway's. He could never cow her by violence, as he cowed his men; on the contrary, he feared her lashing tongue when she was aroused.

He had seen Pierre, Shorty, and Kramer gloating over the gold, and he knew that he would have short shrift if once his men suspected that he was unable to keep it against them, or if they trusted each other sufficiently to combine against him. That was why he had removed it to the hut in the swamp, approachable only by a single narrow track.

There were six other men at the promontory, one of them, the man whom Lee had shot through the hand, being still disabled. Rathway set the whole lot on various jobs, to keep them busy during the remainder of the day. He knew that they would be talking about the gold at night, but he was making his own plans. And, left alone, he paced the track, now gloating over the gold, now over Joyce who still lay silent on the bed, her lips compressed, and that awful look in her eyes.

He went to her side and cut the bonds that bound her. There was no need to guard her; she could not escape him. Joyce sat up slowly, still looking at him in that terrible way. He could not face her eyes; he felt helpless before her. He needed two allies — night and whisky.

'Come, dearie,' he began in a voice that was meant to be placable, 'you know everything I've done has been out of love for you — '

'Murderer!'

Rathway trembled before her outstretched finger. He had thought to have her at his mercy; she seemed to have him at hers.

'Come, now, my dear, if I had to treat you rough — '

'Murderer!'

'He was pulling a gun on me. He fell into the stream himself. I didn't hit him.'

'You — murderer!'

Rathway beat a retreat. Her eyes were blazing like a panther's. He couldn't understand his fear of her. He crossed the neck, went into his hut, and began drinking. His mind was muddled, and worse, his will was wavering. That woman was bad enough — then there would be Estelle to face.

Curse them! The mental picture of Joyce rose up before his eyes. She had never seemed so desirable. He saw her unconscious in the mine again, with her short fair hair hanging about her neck, her eyes closed, helpless. Curse her! Why had he only been thinking of the gold? He had had her at his mercy then.

He looked cautiously into the hut again. Joyce was still sitting on the bed, still as a carven statue. Rathway was beginning to be afraid that she was going mad. If she would only give him the chance, he wanted to tell her that he would share the gold with her. Why couldn't she be reasonable? It was that damned Anderson! How long would she be thinking of him? Weeks, perhaps.

His suspicions of Joyce and Anderson lashed him, and he raged all the afternoon, abusing his men, giving them unheard-of tasks. He had the boats cleaned, the engine overhauled, a drum of gasoline placed in the motorboat. He sent some food to Joyce. The men grumbled and went about their work sullenly.

Rathway fancied he saw looks passing between them, as if they had some secret understanding. He believed they were conspiring against him.

And where the devil was Estelle? In spite of the hate that he now felt for her, he turned to her in his thoughts in time of difficulty. Curse the woman! She was getting *too strong* a hold on him! He must send her packing.

His desire for Joyce was a constant goad to him. But he was still afraid of her. He must give her time to weaken. It was not dark enough. And he had not drunk enough.

At nightfall the men began a carousal, gathering in a hollow between the huts, protected by a skin roof and sides but open in front, where a huge fire was kindled. Usually Rathway kept liquor from them, except when on long journeys and for the weekly debauch which he permitted, but now they were openly defying his rigid rule. The possession of the gold had disintegrated everything.

For Rathway, too. He cared no longer. The drunker his followers became, the better for the plans that were condensing in his mind.

As he passed, one of the men defiantly held up a bottle, an act that would have brought swift physical retribution under other circumstances. A man at his side dashed it out of his hand, whispering in his ear. The bottle smashed, and the spirit ran out on the ground. Rathway affected not to notice the incident. Another man, staggering out of a hut, lurched past him with a mumbled gibe. Rathway affected not to notice that either. Let the fools weave their halter!

He went into his own hut and swallowed a cupful of whisky. It helped to steady his nerves. He crossed the neck and made his way to the hut where Joyce was. It was nearly dark now, and through the darkness he could see her sitting where he had left her, her hands folded in her lap. Fear of her sprung up in him again, and with the fear unreasoning fury. Hate and love left him neutral for the moment, so strongly they contested within him.

Joyce did not turn her head, and he steered a wide course of the bed, edging sidewise toward the sack of gold dust. Picking it up, he made his way quickly outside. With a great effort he managed to hoist it upon his back, and, staggering along, almost bent double by his burden, he made his way among the reeds until he reached the shore of the lake, a few yards from where the motorboat lay beached at the end of the broken parapet.

He laid the bag down in the swamp growth. He felt more at ease now. No one would think of looking for it there, and to hoist it into the motorboat would be a matter of only a minute or two.

Looking into the boat, he saw that Kramer had placed the drum of gasoline in it, as he had ordered.

Rathway chuckled. Joyce, the boat and the gold — and Estelle away! What more was needed?

A few hours' delay, until the men were

stupefied with whisky, then . . .

One minute's start was all he needed. Then he was safe. He could make Lake Misquash in three days. There, in the far north, at the last outpost of the Free Traders run by a man whom he supplied periodically with hooch for sale, he would remain with Joyce, safe against pursuit through the long winter. In any event, it was not likely that the gang would have the enterprise to follow him.

In spring, Joyce and he would move south by other trails. By spring she would have forgotten Anderson.

It was beginning to snow again. Clouds would cover the moon that night. Things could not have turned out more favorably. Best of all was Estelle's absence.

But then, through the failing twilight, Rathway saw her coming toward him along the path through the reeds.

And a fury of resentment rose in his breast at the sight of her. He had never hated her more. Why had he tolerated this woman so long after she had ceased to mean anything to him? There was murder in his heart as he advanced to meet her.

18

Lee is Given a Powerful Tool

It was dawn in the gorge when Lee opened his eyes. At first his memories were confused so that he could carry them no further forward than the moment when he turned away from the log house, leaving Joyce with Rathway.

He had meant to kill him then — and here he must have fallen asleep in the forest, for it was daylight. And Joyce had been all night in Rathway's power!

Murder filled his heart; and again everything else was blotted out of his mind but the insensate desire to slay, a primal instinct that swamped every other part of the man's being.

He started up. But — this was not the forest! He was amazed to see the walls of the gorge on either side of him, dwindling away in the distance into open country with a vista of trees beyond, and splashes of sunshine interspersed with long waves of shadow showing that the sun had already risen.

Almost immediately beneath the ledge on which he lay was a cataract, but not deep — a roaring stream of water rushing among the rocks. And not far away was old Leboeuf, placidly frying bacon in a skillet over a wood fire.

Then all the events of the night flashed into Lee's mind. He uttered a cry and got on his legs.

'Leboeuf!'

At Lee's cry, the old Indian turned and came toward him, the skillet in his hand. 'Monsieur?'

'We must go back. Joyce — ' And he began to tell the old man of the events of the night, that Joyce and he were married — but it was all incoherent, and he was not sure that he succeeded in making Leboeuf understand.

But if Leboeuf did not quite understand what Lee was trying to tell him, he understood enough to send him into a flaming fury. He shook his fists. He danced. His face grew red with blood.

'We must save her, Leboeuf,' Lee exclaimed.

'We must go at once, monsieur. But one cannot return that way. There is only one way into the mine beneath the stone. No one can breast this river. I shall show you. But wait!' He disappeared within a small cavern in the mountain, and reappeared in a moment or two carrying a rifle. 'Now, monsieur, there is no time to lose. I shall pick them off one by one as they come out of the house. Eh, my little Joyce in the hands of that devil! But my master has shown me in a dream that she shall not be harmed. Still, it was the last words my master spoke to me while he was alive, that I should protect her from him, and he has warned me many times in dreams also. Eh, this way, monsieur!'

Lee, feeling recuperated despite the throbbing of his bruised scalp, followed the old man along the narrow coping of rock beside the cataract. In a little while the path grew wider and the rocky walls fell back, becoming outlying spurs of the mountains. The roar of the cataract grew faint behind them. They continued down a gentle gradient onto a level plain. The forest closed about them.

Then, when they had been proceeding for about half an hour, the forest suddenly came to an end, and to Lee's amazement, he found himself standing near the bank of the main river which flowed through Siston Lake. He could not have been more than half a mile from the log house.

But they heard the sudden throbbing of the motorboat. Lee ground his teeth. In an instant old Leboeuf had pulled him down behind the shelter of a rock.

Then they heard Joyce scream. Again and again her agonized cries rang out. Lee tried to leap to his feet; he would have flung himself into the river, but the Indian's iron arms encircled him. And, as he tried to cry out in answer, a hand closed over his mouth.

Next minute the motorboat shot into midstream. It contained Rathway and his three aides; there was something huddled in the bottom of the boat, undoubtedly Joyce; and there was no doubt that they were making for Siston Lake. And all the while Joyce screamed, and Lee struggled in the Indian's grasp and tried to cry out, but he could not move or utter a sound.

'Monsieur! Think of her!' Leboeuf was hissing in his ear. 'It is useless to betray yourself. We do what we can. You understand? You promise?'

And suddenly reason came back to Lee. He nodded and Leboeuf released him.

But the next instant it was Lee who knocked up Leboeuf's hand as the old man was drawing a bead upon the boat, now some hundred yards away from them in the middle of the stream.

Leboeuf looked at him reproachfully. 'Monsieur, I could have killed him. I do not err at the mark.'

Again he was about to take aim, but Lee caught the rifle in his hand. 'No, no, Leboeuf. She must not be left to the mercy of those three men. So long as Rathway lives, there's a shade of hope for her. Don't you understand?'

Comprehension came to the old Indian. He lowered the rifle.

Joyce had ceased to cry out, and in

dumb helplessness the two men watched the motorboat shoot past them and disappear around the curve of the shore. They looked at each other.

'If any harm has come to her,' said Lee, 'I swear that I'll kill Rathway like the hound that he is.'

'Good!' Leboeuf nodded vigorously. 'Some men are like the carcajou, monsieur. Yes, he must die. He has done harm enough for one man, and I think *le bon Dieu*, who is so patient, has grown weary of him. But what will you do now, monsieur?'

'Go to Siston Lake. Take her away or die there.'

'Very good, monsieur. That was my own plan also. But it is a journey of a night and a day, and it is necessary to eat, and also to take food with us.'

Lee was for starting immediately, but Leboeuf persuaded him. They were to return to the log house to see if any provisions had been left behind. If not, they were to go through the mine and to Leboeuf's den in the rocks, which could be reached by fording the edge of the subterranean stream. It gave access in one way, but not in the other. And Leboeuf's decision proved a fortunate one, for at the door of the log house they met Father McGrath, his rifle across his back.

'Thank God I've found ye, Anderson!' he cried. 'I couldna sleep all the night for troublin' about ye and that poor lassie. So before the dawn I started off to make sure that no evil thing had happened beyond what couldna be avoided. But what has happened, and where is she, and that band of skunks?'

Lee told him as concisely as possible while old Leboeuf, bustling inside the house, brought out some flour and bacon that the gang had left behind, and proceeded to prepare a meal. Father McGrath listened, uttering sharp expletives which sounded remarkably like clipped oaths deprived of their harmful characteristics by the alteration of an occasional consonant.

'Aye, and I'm no surprised,' he said. ''Tis but what I'd have expected. But still, what can ye do, Anderson? The law's the law, whether of God or man, and that compact ye made with Rathway has no bindin' power.'

'I can arrest him for attempted murder.'

The priest laid a hand on his shoulder. 'Ye canna do that, lad,' he answered. 'There's no court in the land would convict him. In the first place, though ye meant only to save the lassie from him, there's no jury would believe it. They'd say that compact by which ye were to get his wife for the mine stinks in the sight of heaven. Aye, and they'd say ye arrested him to get the woman. Aye, and, furthermore, ye canna shame her by bringin' her into court as a witness. No, lad, ye'll have to let it go. Ye fought a good fight for her, but there's nothing more to do. Nor can ye arrest him for hootch-sellin', for that would be mixin' up public duty with private vengeance. Ye'll see it, lad, when ye grow cool.'

The shrewd, hard common sense seemed to turn Lee's heart to stone. He knew Father McGrath was right. There was nothing he could do. He could not even attempt the arrest of Pierre and

Shorty for the dynamiting without bringing the whole story into publicity. And he knew well enough that, *prima facie*, it looked simply like an attempt on his part to possess himself of the wife of another man. Then there was the discredit that such a case would bring on the police.

But as he stood there, feeling his last hopes gone, Leboeuf laid down his skillet and came toward them. The old man had overheard all that had passed.

'Listen, messieurs,' Leboeuf said, 'now I can tell you what I know. I have known Jim Rathway under many other names, since when he was young man he first came into this district to sell drink to my people. Many years have gone by — twenty years — since he came to Lake Misquash, where my people had their tepees. He was a friend to us. He trapped, and, if he sold a little whisky that was between ourselves, you understand. And he was my friend.

'One day we both start to take the furs from our trap lines. His line runs east and mine runs west. I leave my woman in my tepee. A young wife, messieurs, much younger than myself. In one week I return. My tepee is empty. My woman is gone. So, too, my furs.

'Later I learn she has gone with Rathway. He keep her six weeks. Then he drive her away into the forest. She dare not return to her own people. So she go south to the cities of the white people. Long I search for her, but I never find her. You know what happens to our women in the cities of the white men, messieurs.

'Then my heart becomes hard, like a stone. As for her, she is nothing to me now. But someday I find Rathway again, and then I kill him.

'Well, messieurs, many years ago I come here. I work for my master, Mr. Pelly. He trusts me. He tells me the secret that he has come here to hide. He shows me the mine that he has found. And for years we work it together, taking out the gold. He want me to take a share, but gold is nothing to me, now that I have the revenge in my heart. It shall be all for him, and Mam'zelle Joyce someday.

'Then Rathway comes. My people have

caught him doing another such a wrong, but my master tells them to forgive, and because they love my master, they do not injure him. So the peace is laid upon me also.

'But I tell my master what Rathway did to my woman, and he turns back in time to save Mam'zelle Joyce from him. He shoots him through the arm. And Rathway smiles and tells him he has learned the secret that can bring my master to die.

'After that, my master is as his servant. And again I say, let me kill him, and again my master says no. And he obeys Rathway in fear, only he would never show him the mine, which is for Mam'zelle Joyce.

'Night after night Rathway follows us, but always he loses us at the rocking stone, for he cannot come near enough to discover the secret without being seen. Then Mam'zelle Joyce goes away to school, and after that Rathway gives my master no peace. And at last he betrays him, thinking that when my master has been hung for the murder, the mine becomes Mam'zelle Joyce's, and he will marry her and it will be his own.

'And so a policeman comes here — that was during the war. But my master could not be found, for he was dead already. You see, messieurs, Rathway thought perhaps he would not be hung after all, since it was so long since my master killed his enemy, and so the mine would not be his; and so — he murders him.'

'What's that?' cried Lee, starting toward Leboeuf.

'He kills my master, monsieur.'

'You saw this?'

'Yes, monsieur. It was near the rocking stone. Rathway had followed him and demanded knowledge of the entrance. He threatened him with his revolver. My master drew his and Rathway fired. My master dropped dead. Rathway flung his body over the cliff into the mine not knowing that it was the mine. He thought that it would never be found.'

Lee turned to Father McGrath. 'I'm going to save her now,' he cried exultantly. 'I am authorized to take any necessary action in connection with Pelly's death, and I propose to put Rathway under arrest and bring him into Manistree. Leboeuf, you'll swear in court you saw this murder?'

'I saw it, monsieur, from the tunnel, but I could not have stopped it. And so I hid, lest Rathway should find the entrance. Afterward I was afraid. I am old now, not like I was when Rathway stole my woman from me. I was afraid of him. And my master comes to me in dreams and says, 'Not yet, Leboeuf!''

Lee gripped the old man by the arm. 'Leboeuf, will you come to Siston Lake with me and help me arrest Rathway? We'll both probably get killed, but I'm going if I have to go alone.'

'I will go with you, monsieur,' answered Leboeuf quietly.

'Two of us against six. But — '

'Hang hard, man!' cried Father McGrath. 'Will I be too old, think ye, to help ye arrest that murderous hooch peddler and clean out that nest of skunks with ye?'

'You, Father?'

'Aye, myself,' answered the priest. "'Twas surely a lucky impulse that made me bring this rifle with me. The three of us can render a good account of ourselves.'

'And see, monsieur,' said old Leboeuf, stepping toward the house. He stooped and picked up the rifle Father McGrath had given Lee. Lee had let it fall in the snow the night before when he was surprised by Estelle. The weapon, nearly hidden in the drift beneath the window, had escaped the notice of the gang. Lee opened the breech and found six rounds in the magazine.

'We'll have six round apiece, and if we're prudent, we won't need that many,' said Father McGrath. 'Ye have six in yours, Leboeuf?'

But the Indian had a single-loading rifle, an old Winchester. However, he pulled a handful of cartridges out of his pocket.

'That's good enough,' said Lee.

After packing a little food to suffice them on the journey, they started along the trail. Some little distance from the house, however, Leboeuf showed to Father McGrath and Lee the prints of double horse-tracks, going and returning.

Leboeuf stooped and examined them. 'It is the horse of Rathway's woman,' he pronounced.

And with that, Lee recalled his interrupted conversation with Estelle the night before. 'You don't have to commit murder to get her,' she had said. But Joyce's appearance had broken off their conversation. He wondered what it was that Estelle could have told him, and what it was beyond jealousy of Joyce, that had brought her in Rathway's wake.

Father McGrath turned to him. 'By the way, lad, there's more than six — there's nine or ten of that hell's crew,' he said.

19

Flimsy Bars

Rathway confronted Estelle with bitter hate in his look as she came up to him. 'Well, where have you been?' he demanded roughly.

'What's that to you?' Estelle retorted.

'See here! You think I'm going to have you prowling all around the country, doing God knows what, when I'm keeping you here?' His eyes roamed over her. He saw that her clothes were splashed with muddy snow. He saw the fatigue in her bearing. 'By God, you followed us!' he cried. He seized her fiercely by the wrists. Estelle looked into his face, laughing contemptuously. Rathway's eyes fell. He swore under his breath.

'You think you can frighten me by violence, Jim? You ought to have learned by now that that doesn't pay. Which did you bring back, the woman or the gold?'

Rathway writhed under the sting of her contempt. 'You were eavesdropping outside the house, damn you!' Suddenly he changed his tone. 'Both!' he cried exultantly. 'I've got the woman, and I've cached the gold near here, where no one can find it.' His rage broke out again. 'I've had *enough* of your tongue!' he cried. 'I'll have no spies in my camp. You could put a rope around my neck with what you know. By God, Estelle, a little common sense should tell you you're playing with fire when you try to cross me. I've never treated you mean with money. You'll have enough to live in comfort on for the rest of your life if — '

'What have you done with Anderson?' asked Estelle quietly.

'Anderson's where he'll cause no further trouble.'

'You mean you — you killed him, after — after your agreement?'

'Damn you, you heard that, did you?' shouted Rathway, turning livid with fear. 'No, I didn't kill him, if you want to know. He met with an accident . . . See

283

here, Estelle,' he continued, 'you and me've got to work together on this game and not try to cross one another. Play fair with me and I'll play fair with you. I want you to make that woman act sensible. She's like a tigress. Now you're an intelligent woman. You know how I feel about her, and quarrelling won't help matters. It won't last, and then I'll come back to you.'

Estelle drew her hands out of Rathway's grasp and placed them on his shoulders, looking searchingly into his face.

'Now, Jim, I want you just to listen to me,' she said. 'You know you've never gone wrong when you've followed my advice. And I guess you know I'm the only friend you've got in the world, don't you, Jim?'

'Well, what if that's so?' he muttered.

'I told you you'd made a mistake in bringing that woman here, before.'

'Aye,' he sneered, 'and you told me old Pelly's mine didn't exist. And I've got the gold! I've got the gold, I tell you!' he cried exultantly.

'I was wrong then, but that was a matter of fact and not of judgment. Jim, you know this is nothing but an infatuation of yours. As you said, it won't last. And what are you going to do with her afterward? You know what it'll mean to you.' Estelle was pleading now. 'You know when McGrath learns the truth, he'll raise the whole country against you. Let her go, Jim. What do you mean to do?'

'You know what I mean to do!' snarled Rathway; but he could not meet her gaze.

Estelle laid her hand on his arm. 'Jim, did you ever have pity on anyone in your life?' she asked.

'Oh, maybe, when I was young and foolish.'

'Did you ever feel respect for any woman, Jim?'

'Ah, cut out that line of talk, Estelle! Don't try to ride the moral horse when it's just plain jealousy — one female jealous of another. That's all it is.'

'It's not, Jim. And you'll regret what you're planning to do. I — I feel you're slipping your neck into a noose . . . '

He leaped back and swore violently at her. 'Cut out that talk, I tell you!' he shouted, almost beside himself.

'Jim, listen — just listen. I guess I'm not what anyone would call a good woman, but I was like that woman once, and — I can't bear it. Jim, I'll do anything in the world for you if you'll have pity on her. It may be there's jealousy, too, but it's much more — much more for her sake — and for yours.'

Estelle was working herself into one of her frenzies. Rathway grew crafty. It is not easy for a man to fool a woman, except when she is in love with him. Then it isn't very hard. And Estelle was desperately eager to be deceived.

'See here, Estelle,' said Rathway gently, 'you know if I let her go what would happen. I've got to keep her here till I know there's going to be no comeback. I've got to see this thing through. She'll come to no harm at my hands.'

Estelle looked at him eagerly. 'Jim, you mean that?' she cried. 'You swear that you mean it?'

'I mean more than that. You know me

and you are partners, through thick and thin, for a good while now, though we've had our quarrels. Well, I won't deny what you said about an infatuation. But I'm getting to see things reasonable. And you're my old partner, Stella.'

What a *fool* the woman was — all women were! She was clinging to him, looking up at him with that absurd expression on her face that had once set his heart leaping. How he hated her!

'Jim! If I could dare to believe what you're saying — '

'Oh, I guess you can believe me, Stella,' Rathway answered easily. 'I'll have to keep her here a week or so, just to show McGrath I'm not running away. You see, there's Anderson's accident. He fell down the cliff — killed at once, of course; and if I was to go away now, they'd think there'd been foul play or something.'

'You — you swear it was an accident, Jim?'

'Sure it was! So you see, Stella, I've got to keep her here a little while. Then we'll get away from here forever, you and me, and the gold.'

'Oh, you've made me happier than I've been since — since you seemed to cease to care. You *do* care for me a little, Jim?' she asked, nestling against him.

'As much as ever,' answered Rathway. And, as she twined her arms about his neck, he bent and kissed her. It was the kiss of Judas. But Estelle, happy again to feel her love returned, only lifted her lips to his in a touch that made him wince at his own treachery.

'Then I'll go and stay with that poor woman tonight, Jim, dear,' she said, 'and tell her that there's nothing to be afraid of.'

Rathway, taken by surprise, managed to keep his countenance, but when Estelle had departed for the hut, he broke into almost maniacal curses.

Damn her! She had tricked him with her very innocence!

And once again he found himself in the old predicament: he could take the gold and leave the woman, or he could wait till the opportunity arose to take Joyce, certain that meanwhile his men would demand their shares. Eight of them!

He fell into a gnashing fury. He had risked so much, and this fool of a woman had balked him at the end!

Hour after hour that night Estelle sat beside Joyce in the hut among the reeds, soothing her, mothering her, coaxing her to eat, and trying to restore her tottering mind to sanity.

Hour after hour, Joyce, at her side, sat staring out into the darkness, and did not utter a word.

And hour after hour Rathway sat drinking in his hut on the promontory, and seeking that intoxication that persisted in eluding him, without which he could not shake off the uncertainties that oppressed him.

He must get Estelle out of the way.

The thought of Joyce was unbearable — Joyce, whom he had caught a second time, only to find himself enmeshed in a web of unforeseen things, flimsy, and yet like iron bars between them. If he attacked, Estelle would shrink from nothing. She carried a pistol, too. He dared not stain his hands with another murder. He was afraid of her trust in him, which had disarmed him; and, to be fair with him, he shrank from such a finale to his association with her.

The face of Lee, upturned and white and ghastly in the current, stared at him from the walls, as Pelly's used to do. He shook his fist at it. It drove him out to pace the promontory; then he would return and hurl himself into his chair savagely, and drink again. And again he would fling himself from the hut; and all the while the conflict raged in his soul.

He could hear his men muttering about the fire. They were drunk no doubt, but they had never acted that way in drunkenness before. Something was brewing. He must act that night. He must act soon. He must gag that wild cat, Estelle.

The face of Joyce rose up before his eyes again. He went back, drained his glass, put out his light, he waited a minute till the liquor began to race through his veins, planning what he should do —

'Jim!'

He started. His hands leaped to his

pistol as two shadows glided in through the doorway. Shorty and Pierre advanced openly toward him.

'Stop there!' he growled. 'Well? What d'you want?'

They shifted uneasily in front of him. 'Well, there's been some grumblin' about that gold, Jim,' Shorty vouchsafed. 'The boys kinder seem to think you ain't plannin' to play fair with 'em. They've put Kramer on guard to watch the motorboat in case you might be aimin' to get away with her.'

'What's that?' snarled Rathway.

He sprang to his feet. From the door of the hut, he could discern a shadowy figure near the parapet. For an instant he was about to rush at it in his rage. But then his cunning came to his aid. He turned back into the hut.

'What's their game — and yours?'

Shorty hesitated. 'Well, you see, Jim, me and Pierre's always stood by you, and we kinda thought we'd let you know the boys has been talkin' things over among themselves.'

Rathway smiled sourly. He knew the

pair of them would not have hesitated to side with the mutineers if they had thought there was any chance of outwitting him. Pierre and Shorty knew Rathway's vigilance, his infinite resource.

'Spill it!'

'Well, Jim, I guess they're gettin' ready to rush you, now you've put out your light. They're aiming to tie you up and get away with the gold in the motorboat.'

'Just to tie me? They wouldn't hurt me?' Rathway snickered, and the pair shuffled their feet uncomfortably.

He laughed. And his plans to meet this situation leaped into his mind. He must let the men attack, and then, when he had finished with them, he'd make short work of Pierre and Shorty, and Estelle too. His confidence was coming back.

'They sent me and Pierre to see if you'd gone to sleep here.'

'Well, I ain't,' Rathway returned, laughing again. He knew his nonchalance at once discomfited and bound them to him through fear. 'I've gone to the hut across the neck to say good night to Joyce, and maybe, if she presses me, I won't be hurrying away. Get that?' he asked as they guffawed self-consciously. 'You'll go back and tell 'em I'm gone, Pierre. You got your gun, Shorty? All right. You and me'll have a quiet little session in the swamp, waitin' for 'em to come along the trail one by one — eh, Shorty?'

He clapped each one on the shoulder. 'There's gold enough in that sack to make us three millionaires, and there'll be a damn sight less sharing,' he said. 'And listen, boys. I've cached it, so, if I'm croaked, nobody'll get it. See?'

The men were fools anyway, but trebly so when their cupidity was aroused. Rathway imagined the greed leaping into their eyes, and laughed. He was reckless now. The hooch devil rode him at last. And in his mind's eye he saw the picture.

And, what a holocaust for Joyce! No one could prove anything, either, even if they caught him. And the bodies of Lee and Pelly would never be found. There was Estelle, of course, but whatever happened, she would never give him away. Curiously, Estelle, who had loomed so prominently as his chief difficulty, now assumed an insignificant part in the problem. He didn't even consider what disposition he was going to make of her.

'You get back, Pierre, and say you met me going over to the neck,' he said. 'And hold 'em twenty minutes.'

Pierre departed. Rathway and Shorty went softly out of the hut among the pines. Rathway felt sure enough of his companion to walk in front of him.

They heard the voices of the men about the fire rise into loud declamation as Pierre returned; then the sounds were cut off as they turned along the track through the morass. Presently the stables came into sight above the reeds, and the hut beyond, with a light in it.

'I guess this place will do,' he said to Shorty.

They squatted among the reeds, their pistols in their hands. It had been snowing intermittently through the night, and it was an eerie watch, even for the unimaginative. In the bitter cold and blackness, the night wind rustled the dead stalks of the reeds; the Muskeg, more treacherous for the surface ice that concealed, but could never bind it, stirred and heaved imperceptibly, like a vast sea. Across the neck of land, the flames of the campfire flickered against the rocks.

Suddenly, after what seemed like an eternity of time, Shorty whispered hoarsely in Rathway's ear, pulled at the sleeve of his mackinaw, and pointed. From where they lurked, they could see figures moving against the background of fire in the direction of the neck. Gripping their pistols, they crouched motionless, tense with excitement. But all of a sudden other figures appeared, moving toward the mutineers.

They heard a sharp 'Hands up!' followed by an oath, cries, the discharge of firearms.

And Rathway, trembling like an aspen leaf, stared into Shorty's face.

'It's *him!* He — *he's come back*,' he babbled in superstitious terror.

20

Estelle Betrays Lee

All day, with hardly an interval for food and rest, Lee, McGrath, and Leboeuf pursued their way along the trail toward the Free Traders' headquarters. The Indian went on at a tireless jog. McGrath, with aching, blistered feet, negatived all suggestions for a rest; each stop that Leboeuf, who had taken command, enforced, was maddening to him.

The certainty in Lee's mind of Joyce's fate gave him a superhuman endurance. Twice before, Rathway and he had met; this time he swore that if Joyce had suffered at his hands, he should pay for it with his life, despite his duty to the police.

Night fell, and still they pursued their course through the darkness, until, passing in single file along the track through the morass known to the Indian, they reached the promontory well before morning. As they approached the neck, they saw figures stealing toward them. Thinking that their presence had been discovered, Lee sprung forward with his challenge.

It was the man Kramer who, under the impression that Lee was Rathway, fired as the words left his lips. Lee fired back, both missed, but a bullet from Leboeuf's rifle passed through Kramer's breast, and with a strangling cry the man pitched forward into the lake across the broken parapet.

A scattering fusillade from both sides followed. Then Lee, Leboeuf, and Father McGrath were across the neck among the gang, and laying them about with their rifle butts.

'That's for ye, ye thief!' Lee heard the priest shout, as he felled the tall ruffian with a blow. 'That's for ye, ye swindlin' hooch peddler, mixin' your filthy hooch in with good liquor. And is that yersel', Sweeney? That's what I promised for ye when I caught ye near the mission!'

His rifle stock crashed upon a head.

Father McGrath, in fact, seemed to be mixing in a good deal of private vengeance with the crusade. At every thud a man dropped, and as he smote right and left, ousting his companions from the fray, a sort of war chant broke from his lips.

But the rally was only a momentary one. Having emptied their pistols, Rathway's men streamed away in flight across the promontory, to be brought up and cornered at the further end. Then, at Lee's demand, arms were flung up, and pistols went clattering down.

It was not until now that the gang appeared to realize that it was not Rathway who had turned the tables. The sight of Lee took what spirit remained from them. Two of the men were slightly wounded, two were half dazed by McGrath's blows, and all were injured in one way or another; none of them had any more fight in them.

Lee scanned their faces. 'Where's Rathway?' he shouted.

They exchanged glances. Willing as they were to give up their leader, with or without compensation, the same thought had occurred simultaneously to each of them, that to betray Rathway meant giving up all chances of a share in the gold. And as long as the hut remained undiscovered, that chance always existed.

Impatient of their evasion, Lee dashed out of the hut into which Leboeuf, McGrath and he had herded them, searching for Joyce. He ran into the hut adjacent, then raced across the promontory to the huts near the neck, but Joyce was not in either of these.

There remained the central storehouse, and, running toward it, Lee dealt a succession of furious blows against the door with his rifle stock. It cracked, splintered and fell off its hinges.

McGrath was at his side. The priest struck a match, and by the light of the tiny flare it could be seen that the interior of the place was empty.

Lee swung his rifle butt furiously, knocking over barrels and boxes in the vain hope that Rathway, at least, was hiding behind them. But he was not there. Shaking off the priest, who sought to detain him, Lee ran back to the hut in which the men were herded.

'Where is she?' he shouted, levelling his rifle at Pierre's face.

'In the hut across the neck,' Pierre bubbled, gray with the terror of death.

Lee ran back across the promontory once more, heedless of his companions' shouts behind him. He dashed along a little trail that ran into the heart of the reeds, flinging the dry stalks right and left, as one parts a hanging screen of beads.

For a few moments he felt the ground hard beneath his feet. Then the little path ended. He trod on quaking Muskeg. He pushed on. Again a path seemed to open before him. Again it closed. The head-high reeds were all about him now, the Muskeg held him, and he went floundering in the mud like a mired caribou.

He struggled on, sometimes sinking knee deep in the swamp. He dashed his rifle against the rattling reeds, swinging it around and around his head in the effort to beat them down and discover what lay before him. But they rose resilient from the ground like armed enemies, and in the dark he could see nothing.

He shouted Joyce's name, and now, bewildered, he began to circle blindly on his tracks among the reeds, dashing them down as if they were human enemies. Yet all the while, though he was ignorant of it, chance was directing him circuitously toward the hut in which Joyce sat.

Rathway, the moment that he recovered from the shock of hearing Lee's voice at the head of the attack, hurried to the cabin. Estelle met him.

'Put out that light!' Rathway snarled. 'It's him!' he half whispered. 'And I thought he was dead! Listen to me, now!' he began talking swiftly under his breath.

Estelle crept closer to him. She listened as if he hypnotized her. 'You mean that, Jim? You swear to leave that woman behind?'

'I swear it, Stella. I've got the gold cached near the motorboat Everything's ready, and I've had a fresh drum of gasoline put in.'

They heard Lee calling again.

'Now, Stella!' Rathway whispered.

Stella slipped from the hut and hurried a little distance along the path.

Lee, struggling in the swamp, suddenly heard Joyce imploring close at hand out of the darkness, in a voice of anguish: 'Lee! Lee! Come to me! Help me!'

'Joyce! Joyce! It's Lee!'

Suddenly he stopped. The instinct of treachery came to him before he realized that this was not Joyce who called . . . Estelle the mimic, Estelle with Joyce's voice, luring him to destruction.

Out of the dark, a blow descended on his head, sending him reeling forward. He struggled in Rathway's arms. Fiercely they fought in the cabin doorway.

Then Lee was seized from behind. A kick behind the kneecap sent him sprawling on the floor. He felt himself being pinioned. A noose was slipped about his neck, strangling him until he was no longer capable of resistance. Ropes were fastened around his body and legs. A gag was thrust in his mouth. He was helpless as a trussed chicken.

Then the room leaped into light, and

he saw Shorty fastening the ends of the rope to a beam, and Rathway standing over him.

A moan came from Joyce's lips, and her body strained against its bonds. Rathway looked at her and uttered his hyena laugh.

Taking the lighted candle from the table, he set it down in a hole beneath the sill. A thin coil of smoke quickly began to spread upward. Within minutes, the tinder-dry thin boards of the hut were covered with running flames. Smoke began to fill the interior.

Rathway waited till he was sure the hut was well alight, then he slashed the bond that tied Joyce to the bed, picked up the struggling woman, and carried her down the path as easily as a child, in spite of her resistance. As he neared the neck, a spire of flame shot up from the hut behind him.

He was halfway to the water when a figure, silent and tense as a cat, leaped at him from among the reeds. It was Leboeuf, tracking Lee. Rathway, by instinct alone, sprang sidewise just in time to save himself. Leboeuf fell sprawling in the morass.

Estelle and Shorty were waiting beside the motorboat among the reeds. Rathway had reached the side of the boat before Estelle recognized Joyce in his arms. She sprang toward him with a cry. But Rathway coolly placed Joyce in the bottom, and quickly fastened the ends of the rope about the seat. The boat, wedged in the sand, only tilted a little as Joyce struggled.

'Jim, what does it mean? You swore — you *swore* you'd leave her in the hut,' screamed Estelle frantically.

Rathway swore at her. She ran at him like a fury, and he dealt her a blow in the face that struck her to the ground.

She got up dazed, staggered toward him, and stood still as the bright spire of light burst upward from the burning hut. At the same instant, a single pistol shot came from the end of the promontory, followed by a sudden outcry.

'Hold that damn she-wolf for a moment, Shorty,' said Rathway coolly; and, as Shorty threw himself upon

Estelle, who had begun to scream frantically again, he turned aside, found the bag of gold, and, lifting it in his arms, staggered to the boat, and with a mighty heave raised it over the gunwale and placed it in the bottom. Then he pushed the motorboat into the water.

The shouting on the promontory broke into a yell. Figures came running toward them; then, at Estelle's screams, broke and doubled back again. Only Rathway had seen — not Shorty, wrestling with Estelle.

'W-what'll I do with her?' Shorty gasped.

Rathway regarded the pair complacently. Everything was his; one instant now and every care would have fallen from his shoulders. And there was that damn woman screaming!

Shorty dealt Estelle a blow that sent her staggering back. He swung around to Rathway.

'Goodbye, Shorty,' said Rathway softly, and shot him through the head.

The body tottered and dropped at Estelle's feet. Rathway leaped into the boat, pushing it from the shore. As Estelle ran into the water, he felled her with an oar.

The next moment he was at the engine, and the *put-put* began. The boat shot out into the lake. The rattle of the motor was like music in Rathway's ears. He held the craft steady without difficulty against Joyce's incessant efforts to overturn it. Seeing that she had too much leeway, he stooped and tightened the rope that bound her to the seat.

On the margin of the lake, Estelle stood with arms raised to the brightening sky, screaming as if she were demented. Suddenly she turned and disappeared among the reeds that fringed the shore.

Behind the promontory, the hut was going up in a vast sheet of flame. Rathway chuckled. All his fears had disappeared forever. He looked at Joyce, who was now lying quiet in the bottom of the boat. He looked at the gold. The woman *and* the gold! He said that over and over. Already he was far out upon the breast of the lake, and the promontory was dwindling behind him.

He looked at the drum of gasoline in the bow, tried to lift it, and assured himself that it was full. He smiled. Nothing could thwart his plans. He bent over Joyce.

'It's all ended, dearie,' he said. 'Soon as you nod to show you're willing to work with me, I'll unfasten you.'

Joyce did not nod, and he continued: 'You know I don't want to hurt you, my dear. Just nod to show you won't try to upset the boat, and I'll set you free.'

Joyce took no notice. Rathway took the gag out of her mouth. But, though he had been prepared for an outburst of invective such as he would have expected from Estelle, she did not utter a word.

Rathway knew the navigation of every river and stream within a radius of a hundred miles. As his motorboat shot down the short arm of the lake, the promontory disappeared from view. And it seemed to him that a long chapter in his life was closed forever.

He spoke to Joyce again, and perhaps a little element of unselfishness in the man made his appeal pathetic. 'Joyce, if you'll let me unfasten you and not try to upset the boat, I — I promise you I'll not harm you or try to touch you — not till you want me to.'

But Joyce made no response, and Rathway, perplexed, loosened her bonds sufficiently to protect her from injury to the circulation, without enabling her to take any rash action unexpectedly. She took no advantage of this, but lay with her blazing eyes fixed full upon his face. Rathway grew more uncomfortable. He could not bear to meet Joyce's eyes.

And, ironically, in the midst of his triumph there came to him memories of other days — happy days — with Estelle, in the first flush of their union. She had betrayed another man to go to him, but she had never betrayed him. They had loved each other. Even Rathway had loved. For the first time, he thought almost with a pang that he would never see Estelle again.

He looked about him at the eternal forest, drooping from the uplands toward the brink of the lake. He was already safe. There was a trail along the lake's edge, but it was impossible for anyone to catch up with him — if there were anyone to follow — for two hours yet.

He drove the motorboat ashore. He put his equipment on the bank. He collected wood to cook some food. He stooped over Joyce and raised her in his arms to carry her ashore. She offered no resistance now; only her eyes, blazing with scorn, stared steadily into his. And with a new excess of passion, he crushed her to his breast.

'You little devil!' he whispered. 'You had me scared. And I love you all the more for it!' Then, lifting up his eyes, Rathway saw something that sent all his dreams and hopes crushing to the ground.

Half a mile distant, topping a little bare space among the trees, he saw two riders trotting along the trail toward him. At that distance it was impossible to distinguish them.

He set Joyce down, and, looking at them, burst into furious oaths. His horses! Yes, he had forgotten them! Two riders — and how many more men had that damn Anderson brought with him?

Hastily he carried the unresisting woman back into the boat, threw in the utensils that he had taken out for the meal, and started the engine again. Soon the boat was cutting its way downstream once more. It was going faster than any horse could follow.

He looked at Joyce, lying quiet in the bottom of the boat. She was no longer looking at him. She had fallen asleep. A slight smile hovered about her lips. It frightened him, that smile; it was as if in her sleep she communed with some protecting force that assured her of safety.

And suddenly his heart was filled with superstitious fears. This woman seemed unbreakable. He thought of Estelle's words. And now he wished that he had taken her advice and let Joyce go.

About the middle of the afternoon he ran ashore again, gathered more firewood, and cooked a meal, eating ravenously. He tried to make Joyce eat, but she lay still in her bonds, ignoring him. When he kissed her, her lips were cold as ice.

He cut her bonds. He drew her into his arms. The touch of her unresisting body against his own restored his courage.

'Joyce!' he cried. 'Joyce! I've got you now! You're mine.'

She was not looking at him. She was looking past his head and smiling. Involuntarily, Rathway turned his head to see.

A mile away, on the shore of the lake, he saw the two horsemen riding steadily toward him.

Furious oaths burst from his lips. At that moment he seemed to read his doom. It was incredible that they could have ridden so fast. He must go on and on now, on till he had pitted the last ounce of his machine fuel against horse flesh — and won. Once more he carried Joyce back into the boat. Once more he hurled his craft downstream.

An hour passed. The sun was beginning to decline. And now out of the far distance a faint murmur broke upon his ears. Rathway knew what it was; he had often heard it before. It was the roar of Reindeer Falls. Beyond those there was no trill — nothing but impenetrable forest through which no horse could pass. Beyond the rapids he was safe. And he had often navigated them. He knew the narrow channel between the rocks. Once more his hopes revived.

Looking back, he could see nothing but the forest reaching down to the lakeshore. The roar of the rapids grew louder. They appeared in the distance, a line of foam crinkled with the black outcropping of the rocks.

However, the engine began to misfire, and Rathway perceived that the gasoline was almost exhausted. He filled the reservoir from the drum. The engine rattled and stopped. The boat began to drift sidewise with the increasing current.

Rathway examined his engine. He could not discover anything the matter with it. It seemed in perfect order — it would not run, that was all. He raved. He looked about him in despair. He looked back; there was no sign of the horsemen.

Suddenly, as if illumination had come to him, he tilted the drum, poured a little stream of the contents into his hand, and raised it to his nostrils. Then, with a frenzied oath, he raised the drum and hurled it into the lake.

Kramer, to prevent Rathway's escaping with the gold, had emptied the drum of its contents and refilled it with water!

Rathway looked back in his despair and once more saw the horsemen riding on the trail.

21

Saved by Estelle

As the wall of the hut burst into flames, Lee struggled with all his might to free himself of his bonds. But in spite of all his efforts, he could not loosen them an inch. He writhed until the cords drew blood from his wrists, and the thought of Joyce, lost to him at the last through Estelle's trick, inspired him to still more frenzied efforts, but equally in vain.

Suddenly a figure darted through the doorway. In his condition of semi-consciousness, he was dimly aware that Estelle was crouching at his side, trying to unknot the ropes. It was impossible to see anything through the thick smoke that filled the interior of the hut, and Estelle's fingers, groping for the knots, were not strong enough to loosen them.

Still she fought in a frenzy, maddened by Rathway's desertion of her, his blow, and Shorty's murder; hardly knowing why she was bent upon saving Lee when her whole life had gone down in ruin. Two walls of the hut were now in flames, and the whole roof was smoldering. Estelle screamed wildly into the empty air.

Lee tried to push her away. 'Go — never mind me!' he tried to mumble through his gag. And he wondered why she, who had lured him there, was now trying to save him.

She bit at the ropes with her teeth, and even while she did so those screams continued to pour from her lips. At last, with a final, despairing cry, she collapsed at Lee's side.

Another figure staggered over the sill. It was Leboeuf. He came on, a moving pillar of mud. The old Indian, attracted by the fire, and hearing Estelle's cries, had at last succeeded in fighting his way out of the Muskeg. Seeing the two forms dimly through the smoke, he bent down, felt the cords about Lee's limbs and body, and with his knife quickly slashed them asunder. He pulled the gag from Lee's mouth and carried him outside. Estelle staggered out after him. In a few moments the fresh air revived them.

But hardly were they outside the hut when the roof collapsed with a great crash, sending up a spout of sparks and brands. A huge banner of fire waved where the hut had been. The glowing brands, descending, ignited the dead reeds. Lines of fire ran swiftly out into the swamp.

The sound of whinnying and plunging came from the stables, which were now discernible against the brightening sky.

'*Monsieur!*' cried Leboeuf, pointing.

Estelle clung to Lee. '*Wait! Wait!*' she cried.

But even in Lee's misery, the instinct to save the animals came first. He and Leboeuf set off toward the building, staggering through the swamp, while the fiery fingers of the conflagration reached out toward them.

'No! This way!' cried Estelle, running toward them.

She guided them along the little trail. In a few moments, Lee and Leboeuf had unhaltered the animals and led them to safety, the Indian carrying the saddles and bridles over his arm.

At the neck of the promontory, Estelle grasped at Lee again. 'He's gone!' she cried. 'He's taken her to Lake Misquash in his motorboat. Oh, don't you care, that you stand there like that?'

Lee looked at her, despair heavy in his eyes. 'So much,' he answered, 'that I shall follow him to the Arctic ice if necessary. That's why there's no immediate hurry, Estelle.'

Estelle could not understand his calmness. 'He made me deceive you,' she cried. 'He swore to me that he'd take me away with him, leaving her in the hut with you. He said he'd place a knife near you, so that you could see it when it grew light, and would be able to free yourself and her. He only wanted a few minutes' respite. I — I believed him, the perjured liar. He tricked me, and now he's gone forever!'

She broke down in stormy sobs. Lee said nothing. At that moment, when everything seemed lost, and it was impossible to save Joyce from the worst, he could only build up endless schemes for future retribution. He would pursue Rathway, if necessary, not only to the Arctic ice, but to the ends of the earth. But — it was too late! That stunning realization kept him as still and silent as if nothing mattered at all.

All the while these thoughts passed through his mind, he was walking with the others across the promontory. It was growing light now, but they could see no signs of movement in the huts opposite them. Lee quickened his footsteps, oppressed by a vague fear.

Outside the huts, he stopped and uttered a cry.

Father McGrath lay in a huddled heap. Lee threw himself upon his knees beside the old priest, sure that he was dead. He took one wrist.

Father McGrath was very far from being dead. He sat up with electrifying suddenness, and dealt Lee a buffet that knocked him backward. And the flow of language that streamed from his lips was, if not actually objurgate, decidedly picturesque. Then suddenly he seemed to realize where he was. He stared at Lee in dismay, looking wildly around him.

'Where are they? Ah, the — !'

Leboeuf, coming up at this juncture with the two horses, uttered a melancholy grunt at the sight of the old priest with his bloody head, and the prisoners gone. McGrath was in a raging fury.

It was not difficult to piece the story together. When Lee had disappeared into the Muskeg, Leboeuf, knowing that it was impenetrable unless one possessed knowledge of the trails, hastened after him, leaving McGrath in charge of the prisoners. Though McGrath remembered nothing from that moment, it could be gathered that one of them had drawn a concealed pistol and fired, felling McGrath and stunning him. Whereupon, thinking him dead, the whole crew had rushed for the motorboat. But, frightened back by Estelle's screams and the sight of the two men there, whom they believed to be more of Lee's raiding party, they had swarmed down the landing place into the York boats and made good their escape. The whole night's work had gone for nothing.

Lee insisted on examining McGrath's wound, and discovered that it was a mere graze along the temple. The bone had turned the glancing bullet.

'Aye, 'tis the thick head of the McGraths saved me, and 'tis the thick head of the McGraths saved them!' the old man lamented bitterly. ''Twas an evil moment when ye consented to bring me with ye, Anderson!'

Lee tried to console him, but McGrath appeared utterly despondent over his failure. It was in vain Lee told him that he did not need the members of the gang; that it was a good thing, on the whole, that they had got away.

'Father,' said Lee, 'we've got to look the facts in the face. First, there's my duty as a policeman to arrest Rathway for Pelly's murder, however far I have to follow him. He's broken for Lake Misquash, and I'm going to follow him there.

'Then there's Joyce. It's true she's his wife.' Here Estelle tried to interrupt him, but he ignored her. His voice choked for a moment. 'I must eliminate that fact from consideration. I'm going to start as soon as possible, and I propose to ride one of Rathway's horses. If Leboeuf is willing to accompany me, I'll take him as a deputy.'

'Ah, monsieur, I come with you, never fear!' answered Leboeuf, making a clucking sound with his tongue against the roof of his mouth.

And then Lee remembered that Leboeuf had a score of his own to settle with the fugitive, apart from the matter of Joyce.

'See, monsieur!' said the Indian, pointing to two pairs of snow shoes strapped against the saddles. 'I have only to make up two packs from what those men have left behind them in these huts, and we are ready to start together to the top of the world. We ride the horses till they can go no longer. Then we take to the raquettes. And at last we catch him. He cannot escape us. There is no place in the world so small that he can hide in, nor no place so silent that we cannot hear him. My master came to me in a dream and told me so. He told me all that has happened here, but I would not let you know. We catch him by falling water. And she — she shall come to no harm. All this my master told me.'

The wizened, mournful face of the old man lit up with a sombre fire. Lee clapped him on the back. 'Good, Leboeuf,' he said. 'We'll start, then.' He turned to the priest. 'You'll be able to make your way home, Father?'

'Trust me for that, lad!' answered Father McGrath. 'I don't doubt but they'll be anxious for me, and it's little more I can do for you, having bungled the game.'

He would not listen to Lee's encouragements. 'No, no, 'tis a sore end to the night's work,' he said. 'But let us thank God we've cleaned out this nest of snakes, anyhow, even if the serpent's gone. Aye, but ye'll catch him, lad, and save that poor lassie from him,' he continued. He spoke without much conviction. 'Before I go, Anderson, 'tis my purpose to clean out this nest of snakes completely. I'll even empty their barrels of the filthy stuff that they've been mixin' with the good corn, and burn down these habitations.'

Lee looked across the neck, where a dense cloud of smoke from the burning reeds hung over everything. 'Good!' he answered. 'Make a clean sweep of it, Father, so that there'll be no chance of their coming back here at any future time. I guess you'll find oil in the storehouse. Now, Leboeuf, if you're ready — '

Estelle, who had been standing by, vainly attempting two or three times to intervene, came forward, placing her hand timidly upon Lee's arm. 'You — you won't hurt him? You'll promise me to do him no harm, whatever — whatever he may have done?' she pleaded.

'If it's possible, I promise you that I shall take him unharmed back to Manistree,' Lee answered. 'That's my duty; and it will also be my duty to require you as a witness.'

She burst into tears. 'Oh, he isn't altogether bad!' she sobbed. 'Nobody knows the good that's in him.'

Perhaps that was the best tribute that could have been paid Estelle. Lee, struck by a sudden thought, turned to the priest. 'Father, you must take her back to the mission with you,' he said.

'Aye,' said McGrath. ''Twas what I was thinkin' myself.'

'You must go with him,' said Lee, and put his foot in the stirrup.

Estelle clutched at him, and now the look in her eyes was one of resolution. 'Lee — wait! There's something I must say to you! You remember what I was saying to you two nights ago, about it's not being necessary to — to kill him, to get that woman from him?'

Lee only looked at her.

'Lee, I may never see you again. I want you to forgive me for all the wretched, miserable wrongs I did you in the past. If it's any consolation — I know it can be none — but I did love you once. I knew I was unworthy of you, but it wasn't all fake and sham.'

'Never mind, Estelle,' said Lee. 'All that's long past.'

'I should have told you about — about the man, Kean, but I didn't dare to. You — you idealized me. You thought me something that I wasn't and could never have been.'

'Estelle — !'

'If you hadn't put me upon a pedestal, I should have found courage to tell you that Kean had been my lover, and that I cared more for you, then. I should have kneeled at your feet and begged you to forgive me. I ran away with him because I was afraid of you, and I have hated you — and hate you still — because of the wrong I had done you.'

'Please don't say any more, Estelle,' Lee tried to interpose.

'You think that I'm a woman with a score of lovers, and there's only been one man in all my life, Lee. Because — I'll tell you now. Jim Rathway is Kean. And his wife's still alive — at any rate, she was alive when he went through that marriage ceremony with Joyce. Alive and not divorced from him. *That makes Joyce yours!*'

22

Retribution

The cold rage in Lee's heart was like an inexorable demon driving him. Mile after mile they covered, urging their foam-flecked horses along the trail as remorselessly as the resolve in their own hearts drove them.

It was when they topped a bare elevation among the pines that Leboeuf touched his companion's arm and pointed. In the distance Lee saw the motorboat drawn up on the shore. And with that, some instinct told him that Rathway could not escape them, that he would never reach Lake Misquash. Lee burned now with the same faith that animated Leboeuf.

They drove their horses on, and saw the motorboat depart, heard the chug of its engine die away in the distance.

It was about the middle of the

afternoon that Leboeuf touched Lee's arm and pointed a second time. Again Lee saw the motorboat. Again they heard the rattle of the engine swell up and die away. But now, by the same faith, Lee knew that Joyce's deliverance was very near, although their horses were wearied almost to death.

Again they rode on through the afternoon. The Indian, who had not spoken a word since their departure, touched Lee's arm a third time. And now Lee saw the motorboat again, but it was drifting, apparently aimlessly, in the river, and moving slowly toward the rapids. Joyce sat in the middle of it, and Rathway was at the engine. Lee and Leboeuf rode cruelly, drawing out their horses' last reserve of strength.

What was the man doing? They saw him rise and hurl something into the water. He stood up in the boat, he shook his fist at them, and his yells of defiance reached their ears above the roar of the stream.

Then, seizing an oar, Rathway began paddling frantically in the endeavor to get the boat bow on preparatory to guiding her down the narrow course among the rocks.

Lee and Leboeuf were nearly abreast of the boat now — and of a sudden Lee knew that Joyce was his. His, in life and death, forevermore! She saw, she knew him, and their spirits seemed to rush together across the waters.

Without hesitation, Lee and the Indian put their horses into the river. They drove the frightened beasts through the ice-cold water, making a course immediately toward the boat, which was now being swirled by the torrent toward that black chain of projecting rocks.

The horses yielded to the force of the stream. They were being carried away. Lee felt the swift rush of the water past him as he rode, submerged to the waist. He saw Leboeuf a little in front of him. And a wild exhilaration filled his heart, and his whole personality seemed to rush out before him, anticipating his vengeance and his love.

The frightened, snorting beasts were now helpless in the rush of the river, which gathered force momentarily as it drove them toward the rocks. They were hardly a boat's length from where Rathway was striving desperately to right the motorcraft. He was too late, he had not calculated on the force of the current, which slewed the heavy boat around, in spite of Rathway's strongest efforts. One moment of suspense and terror — and the motorboat wedged itself fairly between two upstanding rocks beside the channel's mouth. Such was the velocity of the stream that it drove into its place with a force that fixed it as firmly as if it were a part of the rocks themselves, and clung there, with a swirl of white water around it, reaching almost to the gunwales.

In those last moments Lee saw Rathway, standing in the boat, drag Joyce to her feet and clutch her to him, as if resolved to be united with her at the last. His free hand he extended menacingly toward Lee as he approached, himself spinning upon his whirling mount like a straw in the torrent.

Then Leboeuf had struggled from his

horse's back, poised himself upon the gunwale of the motorboat, and, with a bellow of rage, seized Rathway by the throat. To and fro they rocked; the boat, despite their struggles, remaining firm as a wedge. And now the great shoulders of the old Indian were dragging his enemy from his place.

What Leboeuf said to Rathway in those last moments no one ever knew, for the roar of the rapids drowned all other sound. But all of a sudden, Rathway's resistance seemed to cease. Perhaps in Leboeuf he recognized the advent of that nemesis he had defied; he collapsed, and Leboeuf, holding him in his arms, poised himself one instant on the gunwale.

The next both men had disappeared forever in the surge of the rapids that swept them through the falls, grinding them into unrecognizable pulp along the rocks.

Lee grasped at the boat as his horse swept by to its destruction. He clung there, then clambered in. His arms were about Joyce. She lay there, and they forgot everything in the peace that had descended under the veil of the smoking spray.

It was long before they awakened to realities. They looked about them, smiling at their position. Death seemed so small a thing to them, now. And yet, the boon of life . . . how much it meant!

Lee crept to the bow. The boat, wedged firmly between the rocks, was nevertheless being constantly swept sidewise by the swirl of the current. He came back to Joyce.

'If I could dislodge her, I believe she'd go through that channel in the rapids. Joyce. I — I'll have to try.' Lee's clothes were freezing on him; in the boat were packs, supplies — life, life for both of them if she could take the rapids.

'I'll try, Joyce.'

They held each other for a moment longer. Then, taking the oar, Lee drove the handle into the gap between the rocks and levered with all his strength. The boat began to give. One instant it hung giddily on the abyss; the next it was back in position.

'Lie down, Joyce!' Lee flung all his

strength into that attempt, conscious that life and death trembled in the balance.

The boat gave, clung to the rock, was swept sidewise, righted herself and plunged down the channel to safety in the calm waters below.

★   ★   ★

'Lee, dearest, it's from Father McGrath. He wants us to come up to the settlement this summer. He's got five new Indian babies and he's as proud as punch over them. And Estelle — ' She hesitated and looked at Lee.

'Go on!'

'Estelle's simply devoted to the children, and she's taken up my work with so much pleasure. He says she seems quite happy and he believes in time that she'll forget — him.'

'I might get leave of absence,' Lee mused. 'But with that promise of my commission and our transfer — I think perhaps our visit will have to wait.'

'Someday,' Joyce suggested.

They wondered if that day would ever

come. At times, a longing for the range came over them for those scenes where they had met and loved. But mingled with it were those memories that they had put out of their lives because that shadow must never darken their happiness.

'Someday,' said Lee. 'Perhaps.'

We do hope that you have enjoyed reading this large print book.

Did you know that all of our titles are available for purchase?

We publish a wide range of high quality large print books including:
Romances, Mysteries, Classics
General Fiction
Non Fiction and Westerns

Special interest titles available in large print are:
The Little Oxford Dictionary
Music Book, Song Book
Hymn Book, Service Book

Also available from us courtesy of Oxford University Press:
Young Readers' Dictionary
(large print edition)
Young Readers' Thesaurus
(large print edition)

For further information or a free brochure, please contact us at:
Ulverscroft Large Print Books Ltd.,
The Green, Bradgate Road, Anstey,
Leicester, LE7 7FU, England.
Tel: (00 44) **0116 236 4325**
Fax: (00 44) **0116 234 0205**

YOU CAN'T CATCH ME

Lawrence Lariar

Somewhat against his better judgment, Mike Wells accepts a lucrative assignment from bigtime gangster Rico Bruck. It seems a simple enough job: to board a train and shadow a man on his journey to New York, and then to telephone his whereabouts to Bruck. Mike takes with him the beautiful Toni Kaye, who tells him she wants to escape Bruck's employment and make a career as a singer. But when they arrive at their destination, their target is found murdered . . .

FIRST COME, FIRST KILL

Francis K. Allan

When a mysterious woman visited Gregory Payne, warning him of danger, he dismissed her. Shortly afterwards, he was dead . . . His grieving daughter Linda arrives home with her new husband Walter Gordon, to be greeted by private detective John Storm, who believes Gregory to have been murdered. The dead man left money to various beneficiaries besides Linda — a faithful servant, an old friend, a dissolute cousin, and a steadfast godfather. Could one of them have been moved to strike him down?

SHERLOCK HOLMES:
A STRING TO HIS BOW

N. M. Scott

In these ten meticulously constructed cases, the intellectual prowess of Sherlock Holmes is tested to the utmost. Featuring a suspicious suicide, the mysterious disappearance of a Norwegian princess's jewels while she sleeps through a concert, an investigation of three murders in New England which takes an unexpected turn into alchemy and the Freemasons, a psychic star who claims to be able to reveal the identity of Jack the Ripper, a journey to Wales to investigate the death of a poet, and a stolen Stradivarius violin.

TO DIE FOR

V. J. Banis

Kevin Norton and his friend are Russian agents about to go on a camper trip across Europe and western Asia, bringing support and money to terrorist cells. Their instructions are to take along a group of students, including Gemma and Marianne, as cover, with the ultimate aim of holding Gemma hostage. Gemma's father, a power player in D.C., is suspicious, and hires ex-CIA agent Ben Craig to keep an eye on the girls. Thus begins a long-distance war of nerves, pitting agent against agent, with Gemma's life as the prize . . .